PENGUIN BOOKS

PLUM LOVIN'

No.1 bestselling author Janet Evanovich is the recipient of the
Crime Writers' Association's John Creasey Memorial, Last Laugh
and Silver Dagger awards, as well as the Left Coast Crime's Lefty
award, and is the two-time recipient of the Independent Mystery
Booksellers' Association's Dilys award. She lives in New Hampshire,
where she is at work on her next Stephanie Plum adventure.

To find out more go to www.evanovich.com

PLUM LOVIN'

Janet Evanovich

PENGUIN BOOKS

PENGUIN BOOKS

Published by the Penguin Group
Penguin Books Ltd, 80 Strand, London WC2R 0RL, England
Penguin Group (USA) Inc., 375 Hudson Street, New York, New York 10014, USA
Penguin Group (Canada), 90 Eglinton Avenue East, Suite 700, Toronto, Ontario, Canada M4P 2Y3
(a division of Pearson Penguin Canada Inc.)
Penguin Ireland, 25 St Stephen's Green, Dublin 2, Ireland
(a division of Penguin Books Ltd)
Penguin Group (Australia), 250 Camberwell Road, Camberwell, Victoria 3124, Australia
(a division of Pearson Australia Group Pty Ltd)
Penguin Books India Pvt Ltd, 11 Community Centre, Panchsheel Park, New Delhi – 110 017, India
Penguin Group (NZ), 67 Apollo Drive, Rosedale, North Shore 0632, New Zealand
(a division of Pearson New Zealand Ltd)
Penguin Books (South Africa) (Pty) Ltd, 24 Sturdee Avenue, Rosebank, Johannesburg 2196, South Africa

Penguin Books Ltd, Registered Offices: 80 Strand, London WC2R 0RL, England

www.penguin.com

First published in the United States of America by St. Martin's Press 2007
First published in Great Britain in Penguin Books 2008
5

ISBN: 978-0-141-03540-6

www.greenpenguin.co.uk

I'd like to acknowledge the invaluable assistance of
Alex Evanovich, Peter Evanovich, and my
St. Martin's Press editor and friend,
SuperJen Enderlin.

PLUM LOVIN'

1

Men are like shoes. Some fit better than others. And sometimes you go out shopping and there's nothing you like. And then, as luck would have it, the next week you find two that are perfect, but you don't have the money to buy both. I was currently in just such a position . . . not with shoes, but with men. And this morning it got worse.

A while ago, a guy named Diesel showed up in my kitchen. Poof, he was there. Like magic. And then days later, poof, he was gone. Now, without warning, he was once again standing in front of me.

"Surprise," he said. "I'm back."

He was imposing at just over six feet. Built solid with broad shoulders and deep-set, assessing brown eyes. He looked like he could seriously kick ass and not break a sweat. He had a lot of wavy, sandy blond hair cut short and fierce blond eyebrows. I placed his age at late twenties, early thirties. I knew very little about his background. Clearly he'd been lucky with the gene pool. He was a nice-looking guy, with perfect white teeth and a smile that made a woman get all warm inside.

It was a cold February morning, and he'd dropped into my apartment wearing a multicolored scarf wrapped around his neck, a black wool peacoat, a washed-out three-button thermal knit shirt, faded jeans, beat-up boots, and his usual bad attitude. I knew that a muscular, athletic body was under the coat. I wasn't sure if there was anything good buried under the attitude.

My name is Stephanie Plum. I'm average height and average weight and have an average vocabulary for someone living in Jersey. I have shoulder-length brown hair that is curly or wavy, depending on the humidity. My eyes are blue. My heritage is Hungarian and Italian. My family is dysfunctional in a normal sort of way. There are a bunch of things I'd like to do with my life, but right now I'm happy to put one foot in front of the other and button my jeans without having a roll of fat hang over the waistband.

I work as a bond enforcement agent for my cousin Vinnie, and my success at the job has more to do with luck and tenacity than with skill. I live in a budget apartment on the outskirts of Trenton, and my only roommate is a hamster named Rex. So I felt understandably threatened by having this big guy suddenly appear in my kitchen.

"I hate when you just show up in front of me," I said. "Can't you ring my doorbell like a normal person?"

"First off, I'm not exactly normal. And second, you should be happy I didn't walk into your bathroom when you were wet and naked." He flashed me the killer smile. "Although I wouldn't have minded finding you wet and naked."

"In your dreams."

"Yeah," Diesel said. "It's happened."

He stuck his head in my refrigerator and rooted around. Not a lot in there, but he found one last bottle of beer and some slices of American cheese. He ate the cheese and chugged the beer. "Are you still seeing that cop?"

"Joe Morelli. Yep."

"What about the guy behind door number two?"

"Ranger? Yeah, I'm still working with Ranger." Ranger was my bounty hunter mentor and more. Problem was, the *more* part wasn't clearly defined.

I heard a snort and a questioning *woof* from the vicinity of my bedroom.

"What's that?" Diesel asked.

"Morelli's working double shifts, and I'm taking care of his dog, Bob."

There was the sound of dog feet running, and Bob rounded a corner and slid to a stop on the kitchen linoleum. He was a big-footed, shaggy, orange-haired beast with floppy ears and happy brown eyes. Probably golden retriever, but he'd never win best of breed. He sat his ass down on Diesel's boot and wagged his tail at him.

Diesel absently fondled Bob's head, and Bob drooled a little on Diesel's pant leg, hoping for a scrap of cheese.

"Is this visit social or professional?" I asked Diesel.

"Professional. I'm looking for a guy named Bernie Beaner. I need to shut him down."

If I'm to believe Diesel, there are people on this planet who have abilities that go beyond what would be considered normal human limitations. These people aren't exactly superheroes. It's more that they're ordinary souls with the freakish ability to levitate a cow or slow-pitch a lightning bolt. Some are good and some are bad. Diesel tracks the bad. The alternative explanation for Diesel is that he's a wacko.

"What's Beaner's problem?" I asked.

Diesel dropped a small leftover chunk of cheese into Rex's cage and gave another chunk to Bob. "Gone off the edge. His marriage went into the shitter, and he blamed it on another Unmentionable. Now he's out to get her."

"Unmentionable?"

"That's what we call ourselves. It sounds better than freak of nature."

Only marginally.

Bob was pushing against Diesel, trying to get him to give up more cheese. Bob was about ninety pounds of rangy dog, and Diesel was two hundred of hard muscle. It would take a lot more than Bob to bulldoze Diesel around my kitchen.

"And you're in my apartment, why?" I asked Diesel.

"I need help."

"No. No, no, no, no, no."

"You have no choice, sweetie pie. The woman Beaner's

looking for is on your most-wanted list. And she's in my custody. If you want your big-ticket bond, you have to help me."

"That's horrible. That's blackmail or bribery or something."

"Yeah. Deal with it."

"Who's the woman?" I asked Diesel.

"Annie Hart."

"You've gotta be kidding. Vinnie's on a rant over her. I spent all day yesterday looking for her. She's wanted for armed robbery and assault with a deadly weapon."

"It's all bogus . . . not that either of us gives a rat's ass." Diesel was systematically going through my cupboards looking for food, and Bob was sticking close. "Anyway, bottom line is I've got her tucked away until I can sort things out with crazy Bernie."

"Bernie is the . . . um, Unmentionable who's after Annie?"

"Yeah. Problem is, Annie's one of those crusader types. Takes her job real serious. Says it's her *calling*. So, the only way I could get Annie to stay hidden was to promise her I'd take over her caseload. I suck at the kind of stuff she does, so I'm passing it off to you."

"And what do I get out of this?"

"You get Annie. As soon as I take care of Bernie, I'll turn Annie over to you."

"I don't see where this is a big favor to me. If I don't help you, Annie will come out of hiding, I'll snag her, and my job will be done."

Diesel had his thumbs hooked into his jeans pockets; his

eyes were locked onto mine, his expression was serious. "What'll it take? I need help with this, and everyone has a price. What's yours? How about twenty bucks when you close a case?"

"A hundred, and nothing illegal or life-threatening."

"Deal," Diesel said.

Here's the sad truth, I had nothing better to do. And I needed money. The bonds office was beyond slow. I had one FTA to hunt down, and Diesel had her locked away.

"Just exactly what am I supposed to do?" I asked him. "Annie's bond agreement lists her occupation as a relationship expert."

Diesel gave a bark of laughter. "Relationship expert. I guess that could cover it."

"I don't even know what that means! What the heck is a relationship expert?"

Diesel had dropped a battered leather knapsack onto my counter when he popped into my kitchen. He went to the knapsack, removed a large yellow envelope, and handed it over to me. "It's all in this envelope."

I opened the envelope and pulled out a bunch of folders crammed with photographs and handwritten pages.

"She's got a condensed version for you clipped to the top folder," Diesel said. "Got everything prioritized. Says you better hustle because Valentine's Day is coming up fast."

"And?"

"Personally, I don't get turned on by Valentine's Day, with the sappy cards and creepy cupids and the hearts-and-flowers routine. But Annie is to Valentine's Day what Santa Claus is to Christmas. She makes it happen. Of course, Annie operates on a smaller scale. It's not like she's got ten thousand elves working for her."

Diesel was a really sexy-looking guy, but I thought he might be one step away from permanent residence at the funny farm. "I still don't get my role in this."

"I just handed you five open files. It's up to you to make sure those five people have a good Valentine's Day."

Oh boy.

"Listen, I know it's lame," Diesel said, "but I'm stuck with it. And now you're stuck with it. And I'm going to have a power shortage if I don't get breakfast. So find me a diner. Then I'm going to do *my* thing and look for Bernie, and you're going to do *your* thing and work your way down Annie's list."

I clipped a leash onto Bob's collar and the three of us walked down the stairs and out to my car. I was driving a yellow Ford Escape that was good for hauling felons and Bob dogs.

"Does Bob go everywhere?" Diesel wanted to know.

"Pretty much. If I leave him at home, he gets lonely and eats the furniture."

Forty minutes later, Diesel was finishing up a mountain of scrambled eggs, bacon, pancakes, home fries, and sourdough toast with jam . . . all smothered in maple syrup.

I'd ordered a similar breakfast but had to give up about a third of the way through. I pushed my plate away and asked that the food be put in a to-go box. I drank my coffee and thumbed through the first file. Charlene Klinger. Age forty-two. Divorced. Four children, ages seven, eight, ten, and twelve. Worked for the DMV. There was an unflattering snapshot of her squinting into the sun. She was wearing sneakers and slacks and a sweater than didn't do a lot to hide the fact that she was about twenty pounds overweight. Her face was pleasant enough. No makeup. Not a lot of hairstyle going on. Short brown hair pushed behind her ears. The smile looked tense, like she was making an effort, but she had bigger fish to fry than to pose for the picture.

There were four more pages in Charlene's file. Harvey Nolen, Brian Seabeam, Lonnie Brownowski, Steven Klein. REJECT had been written in red magic marker across each page. A sticky note had been attached to the back of the file. THERE'S SOMEONE FOR EVERYONE, the note read. I supposed this was Annie giving herself a pep talk. And a second sticky note below the first. FIND CHARLENE'S TRUE LOVE. A mission statement.

I blew out a sigh and closed the file.

"Hey, it could be worse," Diesel said. "You could be hunting down a skip who thinks it's open season on bounty hunters. Unless you really piss her off, Charlene probably won't shoot at you."

"I don't know where to begin."

Diesel stood and threw some money on the table. "You'll figure it out. I'll check in with you later."

"Wait," I said. "About Annie Hart—"

"Later," Diesel said. And in three strides he was across the room and at the door. By the time I got to the lot, Diesel was nowhere to be seen. Fortunately, he hadn't commandeered my car. It was still in its parking space, Bob looking at me through the back window, somehow understanding that the Styrofoam box in my hand contained food for him.

The bail bonds office is a small storefront affair on Hamilton Avenue, just a ten-minute drive from the diner. I parked at the curb and pushed my way through the front door. Connie Rosolli, the office manager, looked up when I entered. Connie is a couple years older than me, a couple pounds heavier, a couple inches shorter, a lot more Italian, and consistently has a better manicure.

"You must be tuned in to the cosmic loop this morning," Connie said. "I was just about to call you. Vinnie's bananas over Annie Hart."

Vinnie's ferret face appeared in the doorway of his inner office. "Well?" he asked me.

"Well what?"

"Tell me you've got her locked up nice and neat. Tell me you've got a body receipt."

"I've got a lead," I told Vinnie.

"Only a lead?" Vinnie clapped his hands to his head. "You're killing me!"

Lula was on the faux leather couch, reading a magazine. "We should be so lucky," Lula said.

Lula is a 180-pound black woman crammed into a five-foot, five-inch body. At the moment, she was wearing a red skin-tight spandex T-shirt that said KISS MY ASS in iridescent gold lettering, jeans with rhinestones marching down side seams that looked like they might burst apart at any minute, and four-inch high-heeled boots. Lula does the office filing when she's in the mood, and she rides shotgun for me when I need backup.

"What's the lineup look like?" I asked Connie.

"Nothing new. Annie Hart is the only big bond in the wind. It's always slow at this time of the year. All the serious crackheads killed themselves over Christmas, and it's too cold for the hookers and pushers to stand on the street corners. The only good crime we've got going on is gang shooting, and those idiots get held without bond."

"It's so slow Vinnie's going on a cruise," Lula said.

"Yeah, and the cruise isn't cheap," Vinnie said. "So get your ass out there and find Annie Hart. I'm not running a goddamn charity here. I take a hit on Hart's bond, and I'll have to fake a stroke and cash in my cruise insurance. And Lucille wouldn't like that."

Lucille is Vinnie's wife. Her father is Harry the Hammer, and while Harry might understand about the need for the occasional illicit nooner, he definitely wouldn't be happy to see Lucille get stiffed on the cruise.

"It's one of them champagne Valentine's Day cruises," Vinnie said. "Lucille's got her bags packed already. She thinks this is going to rejuvenate our marriage."

"Only way it'll rejuvenate your marriage is if Lucille brings handcuffs and a whip and Mary's little lamb," Lula said.

"So sue me," Vinnie said. "I've got eclectic tastes."

We all did a lot of eye rolling.

"I'm out of here," I told Connie. "I'll be on my cell if you need me."

"I'm going with you," Lula said, grabbing her Prada knockoff shoulder bag. "I'm feeling lucky today. I bet I could find Annie Hart right off."

"Thanks," I said to Lula, "but I can handle it."

"The hell," Lula said. "Suppose you gotta go into some cranky neighborhood, and you need some muscle. That would be me. Or suppose you need to make a doughnut choice at that new place on State Street. That would be me, too."

I cut my eyes to Lula. "So what you're saying is that you want to test-drive the new doughnut shop on State?"

"Yeah," Lula said. "But only if you need a doughnut real bad."

Fifteen minutes later, I cruised away from Donut Delish and headed for the DMV.

"I can't believe you're not eating any of these doughnuts," Lula said, a bag of doughnuts resting on her lap. "These are first class. Look at this one with the pink and yellow sprinkles on it. It's just about the happiest doughnut I ever saw."

"I had a huge late breakfast. I'm stuffed."

"Yeah, but we're talking about primo doughnuts here."

Bob was in the cargo area of the Escape. His head was over the backseat, and he was panting in our direction.

"That dog could use a breath mint," Lula said.

"Try a doughnut."

Lula flipped Bob a doughnut. Bob caught the doughnut midair and settled down to enjoy it.

"Where the heck are we going?" Lula wanted to know. "I thought we were going after Annie Hart. Don't she live in North Trenton?"

"It's complicated. I had to make a deal. Annie Hart is inaccessible until I wrap up her caseload."

"Are you shitting me? And what's that mean anyways? Does that mean you're taking on her customers? Personally, I can't see you doing that. I read her file. She said she was a relationship expert, and I figured that's code for 'ho."

"It's not like that. It's more like matchmaking. First person on my list is Charlene Klinger. She's forty-two and divorced, and we need to find her true love."

"Oh boy, true love. That's a bitch. You sure she wouldn't be satisfied if we just found her some nasty sweaty sex? I got a couple names in my book for that one."

"I'm pretty sure it has to be true love."

2

Charlene Klinger was behind the counter at the DMV, working the registration-only line. She was prettier in person. Her hair still lacked style, but it was thick and glossy and suited her. Her face was animated, and she smiled a lot. After thirty-five minutes, Lula and I had inched our way up to her. I introduced myself to Charlene and explained I was substituting for Annie Hart.

"That woman is a nut," Charlene said. "I don't know where she came from, but good riddance if she's gone. And I don't need a substitute nutcase. I'm doing fine. I don't want a man in my life. I've got enough problems."

"Didn't you hire Annie?"

"Heck no. She just popped into my kitchen one day. Happens to me all the time. The kids leave the door open and next thing I know, some half-starved cat's wandered into the house and won't leave."

"I was under the impression you wanted to find your true love," I said to Charlene.

Charlene looked at the powdered sugar that had sifted

onto Lula's chest. "I'd sooner find a bag of doughnuts. Don't have to shave your legs to enjoy a bag of doughnuts."

"Amen to that," Lula said.

"You're going to have to move along if you don't want to register something," Charlene said. "You hold up the line too long and this crowd will get ugly."

Lula and I left the building and hustled to my car. It was freezing cold, and we walked with our heads tucked down against the wind.

"Now what?" Lula wanted to know.

I slid behind the wheel and pulled another file out of the envelope. "I have more."

Lula picked a doughnut out of the bag. "Me, too."

"Yesterday you told me you were going on a diet."

"Yeah, but it's something new. It's called the afternoon diet. You get to eat all you want until noon. Then the diet starts."

"Next up is Gary Martin. Runs a vet clinic on Route 1. Never been married. Looks like a nice guy." I passed his picture to Lula.

"He looks like a dork," Lula said. "He's wearing a bow tie, and he's got a comb-over. He don't need a matchmaker. He needs a woman with scissors."

I put the car in gear and rolled out of the lot. "According to Annie's file, he needs help getting his girlfriend back."

"And we're gonna help him? Excuse me if I'm a skeptic, but it don't seem to me we're all that good at relationships. I only date losers, and you have commitment issues. Plus, you can't even make up your mind about who you want as your commitment recipient. You're double-dipping with Morelli and Ranger."

"I'm *not* double-dipping."

"You're *mentally* double-dipping."

"That doesn't count. Everyone mentally double-dips. Keep your eyes open for Municipal Animal Hospital."

The Municipal Animal Hospital waiting room was bright and cheery and sparkling clean. And it was empty of patients. A young woman sat behind the big wraparound desk. She was also sparkling clean, but she didn't look all that cheery.

"Yo," Lula said to her. "I'm Lula, and this here's the world-famous Stephanie Plum, and we're looking for Gary Martin."

"He's in surgery," the woman said. "Office hours start at one o'clock."

"Maybe he could squeeze us in between surgeries," Lula said. "It's a personal matter."

"Dr. Martin doesn't like to be disturbed when he's in surgery."

"See, here's the thing," Lula said. "I got a doughnut with my name on it out in the car, and I don't want to sit around until one o'clock. I mean, it's not like ol' Gary's doing open heart. He's cutting the balls off a cat, right?"

I pointed stiff-armed to the door. "Out," I said to Lula.

"Just trying to communicate with Miss Stick-up-her-ass," Lula said.

"Out!"

I waited until Lula left, and then I turned to the receptionist. "Maybe I could leave a note for Dr. Martin."

There was a long awkward pause, and I assumed the receptionist was contemplating hitting the police button on the security system . . . or at the very least unleashing Dobermans from a holding pen. This was a vet office. They had dogs, right?

Finally, the woman exhaled and slid a pad and pen my way. "I guess that would be okay," she said.

I was halfway through the note when Gary Martin emerged from a back room and approached the receptionist.

"Any emergency calls?" he asked her. "Any, um, personal calls?"

She shook her head, no.

"Are you sure? Not a single personal call?"

Gary Martin looked like a big, forty-year-old cherub. He was about five foot six with chubby cheeks and a soft middle. He was wearing a light blue lab coat that was unbuttoned over tan slacks and a yellow button-down shirt. He was entirely adorable in a dorky kind of way. And he was clearly disappointed that no one had called.

I stuck my hand out and introduced myself. "Annie Hart is temporarily indisposed," I said. "I'm her replacement."

I wasn't sure what to expect after Charlene Klinger, but

Gary Martin seemed excited to see me. He ushered me into his little office and closed the door.

"I've been waiting," he said. "I was expecting Ms. Hart, but I'm sure you're wonderful, too."

"I understand you need help getting your girlfriend back."

"I don't know what happened. Two weeks ago, she just said it was over. I don't know what went wrong. I must have done something terrible, but I don't know what it was. I was going to ask her to marry me on Valentine's Day. And now I don't know what to do. She won't talk to me on the phone, and she won't let me into her apartment. And last time I tried to talk to her she said I was a pest. A pest!"

"I'm curious," I said. "How did you hear about Annie Hart?"

"It was odd. I found her card in my jacket pocket. Someone must have given it to me. It said Ms. Hart was a relationship expert . . . and I thought, that's just what I need! So I called Ms. Hart, and we had a meeting. That was four days ago." Martin took a photo off his desktop and handed it to me. "Ms. Hart wanted a picture of Loretta."

The sticky note attached to the back told me this was Loretta Flack, and Martin had neatly printed Loretta's address and phone number below her name. The front of the photo showed a smiling blond with a Barbie doll shape. It had been taken at some sort of street fair, and she was holding a teddy bear.

"She's a bartender," Martin said. "She works the lunch shift at Beetle Bumpkin. It's a sports bar just up the road. They have good sandwiches at lunchtime, but Loretta said she didn't want me in there anymore."

"She's pretty," I said.

"Yes, she's way too pretty for me. And probably too young. I don't know why she even went out with me in the first place. I thought maybe you could tell her I joined a gym, and I have a private trainer now. And I think my hair is growing back."

I looked up at the three strands of hair plastered to the top of his dome.

"I thought I might have seen some fuzz this morning," Gary Martin said.

"Anything else you want me to tell her?"

"I'll leave it up to you. You're a relationship expert, right? I mean, you know the right things to say."

Oh boy, we were in trouble. I *never* said the right thing. Lula was right. I was a relationship disaster.

"Sure," I told him. "Leave it to me. I'll get this fixed up."

Lula settled her ass on a Beetle Bumpkin barstool and looked around. "Beetle Bumpkin is one of them new mini chains," she said. "There's one just opened downtown. The sandwiches are good because they fry them. Everything's fried. That's the Beetle Bumpkin secret ingredient."

Loretta Flack was taking an order at the other end of the bar. Her hair was yellow under the Bumpkin bar lights, and her breasts were packed into a red Beetle Bumpkin T-shirt. I figured she was maybe fifteen years younger than Gary Martin.

"Let me do the talking this time," I said to Lula.

"My lips are sealed. I'm only here in case you need backup. Like suppose she tries some karate moves or she pulls a gun on you."

"I don't think that's going to happen."

"You never know. Best to be prepared, I always say. People are unpredictable. I learned that in my human be-havior course at the community college. Did I ever tell you I took a human behavior course?"

"Yes."

"It could help in this situation. It's just about qualified me to be a relationship expert. Plus I got a lot of expertise all those years when I was a 'ho. I bet I could relationship the ass off you."

"No doubt. Let me talk anyway."

Loretta made her way down to us. "Ladies?" she said.

"Diet Coke and tuna on rye," I told her.

"I'll have the Beetle special sandwich and cheese fries and a Coke," Lula said.

I looked at my watch. It was twelve-thirty. "What about your afternoon diet?"

"It's more like a suggestion than a rule. And anyway, I

thought since we're working on these cases I should keep my strength up. I might get all weak and hypoglycemic if I don't have cheese fries."

"So," Loretta said. "Working ladies."

"Yep. We're relationship experts," Lula said. "We fix up relationships. You got any that needs fixin'?"

"No. I'm good with relationships. I'm in a dreamy one right now. He's a lawyer."

"You don't look like the lawyer type," Lula said. "You look like . . . some other type."

Loretta drew my drink and slid it down the bar at me. "I'm lots of types. This is a really good job for meeting men. I go out with them and get them to buy me some jewelry and then when it looks like they're gonna say the *L* word I split. I got this necklace I'm wearing from a veterinarian."

"It's a good necklace," Lula said. "And you look like the veterinarian type more than the lawyer type. Maybe you should go back with him."

"He was a loser," Loretta said. "He kept talking about how he wanted a family." She wrinkled her nose. "Eeeuw, kids. Ick. I hate kids. And he was always rushing off to save some dumb cat or dog. I mean, what's with that? Who wants a boyfriend who makes you rush through dessert just because some cat got run over by a dump truck?"

"What a creep," Lula said. "Imagine rushing you through dessert. I wouldn't stand for that."

"The lawyer's a lot better," Loretta said. "He has a wife

and kids, so I don't have to worry about the *L* word. The *L* word is okay if it's insincere."

"Boy, you got it all figured out," Lula said.

Loretta moved off to the other end of the bar.

"What was that?" I asked Lula. "You were supposed to let me do the talking."

"Well excuse me, Ms. Control Freak. It just worked out this way. You weren't taking advantage of the moment."

Turned out it didn't matter a whole lot anyway. I liked Gary Martin, and I hated Loretta Flack. Loretta Flack was bitchzilla. I couldn't in good conscience fix things so that Martin was stuck with Flack.

The sandwiches and fries arrived, and we dug in.

"I'm liking this," Lula said. "We didn't get spit on or shot at all day, and I feel like a big Cupid. Of course, we haven't gotten anybody together like we're supposed to, but it feels like love is in the air. Don't you feel love in the air? How many more cases we got?"

"Three. Next up is Larry Burlew. He's got his eye on someone but can't get to meet her. I've already skimmed the file. Burlew is a butcher. Works at Sal's Meat Market on Broad. The woman of his dreams works in the coffee shop across the street. According to Annie's notes, Burlew is shy."

"That's cute," Lula said. "A shy butcher. I got a good feeling about him. And I wouldn't mind some pork chops for dinner tonight."

3

Larry Burlew was a big guy. He was over six feet tall, weighed maybe 230 pounds, and had hands like hamhocks. He wasn't bad looking, and he wasn't good looking. Mostly he looked like a butcher . . . possibly because his white butcher's apron was decorated with meat marinade and chicken guts.

The butcher shop was empty of customers when we entered. Burlew was the lone butcher, and he was slicing ribs and arranging them in the display case.

I introduced myself as Annie's assistant, and Burlew blushed red from the collar of his white T-shirt to the roots of his buzz-cut hair.

"Real nice to meet you," he said softly. "I hope this isn't too much trouble. I feel kind of silly asking for help like this, but Ms. Hart came into the shop and left her card, and I just thought . . ."

"Don't worry about it," Lula said. "It's what we do. We're the fixer-upper bitches. We *live* to fix shit."

"I understand you want to get together with someone?" I asked Burlew.

"There's this girl that I like. I think she's around my age. I see her every day, and she's nice to me, but in a professional way. And sometimes I try to talk to her, but there's always lots of people around, and I never know what to say. I'm a big dummy when it comes to girls."

"Okay," I said, "give me all the necessary information. Who is she?"

"She's right across the street," Burlew said. "She works in the coffee shop. Every morning I go in to get coffee and she always gets it just right. She always gives me the perfect amount of cream. And it's never too hot. Her name is Jet. That's what it says on her name tag. I don't know more than that. She's the one with the shiny black hair."

I looked at the coffee shop. It had big plate-glass windows in the front, making it possible to check out the action inside. There were three women working behind the counter and a bunch of customers lined up waiting for service. I shifted my attention back to Burlew and saw he was watching Jet, mesmerized by the sight of her.

I excused myself and swung across the street to the coffee shop. Jet was at the register, ringing up a customer. She was a tiny little thing with short, spiky black hair. She was dressed in a black T-shirt, a short black skirt, black tights, and black boots. She wore a wide black leather belt with silver studs, and she had a red rose tattooed on her arm.

She looked to be in her early to mid-twenties. No wedding band or engagement ring on her left hand.

I ordered a coffee. "It's for my cousin across the street," I said. "Maybe you know him . . . Larry Burlew."

"Sorry, no."

"He's a butcher. And he said you always give him perfect coffee."

"Omigod, are you talking about the big huge guy with the buzz cut? He comes in here every morning. He talks so soft I can hardly hear him, and then he goes across the street, and he stares in here all day. I'm sorry because he's your cousin and all, but he's kind of creepy."

"He's shy. And he stares in here because . . . he'd like more coffee, but he can't leave the shop."

"Omigod, I had no idea. That's so sweet. That's so sad. The poor guy is over there wishing he had a cup of coffee, and I thought he was one of those pervert stalkers. He should just call over here. Or he could wave, and I'd bring him a cup."

"Really? He'd love that. He's such a nice guy, but he's always worried about imposing."

Jet leaned on the counter and did a little finger wave at Larry Burlew. Even from this distance I could see Burlew's cheeks flush red.

I brought the coffee across the street and gave it to Larry Burlew.

"I've got it all set," I told him. "All you have to do is wave at Jet, and she'll bring you a cup of coffee. Then you'll have a chance to talk to her."

"I can't talk to her! What would I say? She's so pretty, and I'm so . . ." Burlew looked down at himself. He didn't have words.

"You're a nice-looking guy," I told him. "Okay, maybe the chicken guts are a turnoff, but you can fix that by changing your butcher apron before she gets here. And try not to stare at her so much. Only stare when you want a cup of coffee. Staring sometimes can be misconstrued as, um, rude."

Burlew was bobbing his head up and down. "I'll remember all that. Wave for coffee. Don't stare so much. Change my apron before she gets here."

"And talk to her!"

"Talk to her," he repeated.

I didn't actually have a lot of confidence that this would work, so I wrote my cell phone number on a scrap of paper and left it with him.

"Call me if you have a problem," I said.

Burlew did some vigorous head nodding. "Yes, ma'am."

"Before we go I need to buy some pork chops," Lula said. "I have a taste for pork chops."

Diesel was on the couch watching television when Bob and I got home. There was a six-pack of beer and a pizza box on the coffee table in front of him. Some of the beer and pizza were missing.

"I brought dinner," Diesel said. "How'd it go today?"

"What are you doing here?"

"I'm living here."

"No, you're not."

"Sure I am. I have my shoes off and everything."

"Okay, but I'm not sleeping with you."

"No problemo. You're not my type anyway," Diesel said.

"What's your type?"

"Easy."

I rolled my eyes.

"I'm a jerk," Diesel said, "but I'm lovable."

This was true.

I dragged Bob off to the kitchen, gave him fresh water, and filled his dog bowl with dog crunchies. I returned to the living room, helped myself to a piece of pizza, and joined Diesel on the couch.

"Eat up," Diesel said. "We need to work tonight. I've got a line on Beaner."

"No way. I'm the *relationship* person. I'm not the *find-the-crazy-Unmentionable-nutcase* person."

"I need cover. You're all I've got," Diesel said.

"What makes Beaner special? Can he whip up a tornado? Can he levitate a Hummer? Can he catch a bullet in his teeth?"

"No, he can't do any of those things."

"Well, what *can* he do?"

"I'm not telling you. Just try not to get too close to him."

Bob padded in from the kitchen and stood looking at the leftover pizza. I gave him a piece; he ate it in three gulps and put his head on Diesel's leg, leaving a smear of tomato sauce. Diesel scratched Bob behind the ear, the tomato sauce not worthy of registering on Diesel's slob-o-meter.

It was eight o'clock when I parked my yellow Ford Escape in the small lot attached to Ernie's Bar and Grill. I'd been to Ernie's before, and I knew it was more bar than grill. The grill was mostly wasabi peas and pretzels. The bar was mostly middle-aged white guys who drank too much. It was just one block from the government complex, so it was a convenient watering hole for enslaved bureaucrats who were putting in their hours, waiting for death or retirement, whichever came first. At eight o'clock the bar had emptied out the merely desperate and was left to console the truly hopeless.

"Beaner's been here for two nights running," Diesel said. "He's in there now. I can sense it. Problem is, I can't approach him in a public place. I know he's holed up somewhere nearby, but I can't get a fix on it. I want you to try to get him to talk to you. See if you can find out where he lives. Just don't let him touch you. And don't get too close."

"How close is *too* close?"

"If you can feel his breath on your neck, it's too close. He's five feet, eight inches tall, weighs 180 pounds, and looks late forties. He has brown hair, cut short, blue eyes, and he's got a raspberry birthmark on his forehead that extends into his left eyebrow."

"Why don't you follow him when he leaves the bar?"

"Not an option, unless he leaves with you."

I gave Diesel a *why not* look, and Diesel mumbled something.

"What?" I asked.

"I can't." More mumbling.

"You want to run that mumbling by me again?"

Diesel slumped in his seat and blew out a sigh. "I keep losing him. He's really sneaky. He turns a corner on me, and he's gone."

"The stealth Beaner."

"Something like that. He scrambles my radar."

"You don't actually think you have radar, do you?"

"No, but I have GPS. And sometimes ESP. And Monday nights I get ESPN."

Okay, he was a little nutty, but at least he had a sense of humor. And hell, who was I to say whether or not he actually had ESP. I mean, I sort of believe in ghosts. And I sort of believe in heaven. And I sort of believe in wishing on birthday candles. I guess Diesel and ESP aren't too far removed. Sort of in the area of radio waves, spontaneous combustion, and electricity. After all, I don't understand any of those things, but they exist.

"Sometimes you just have to go with it," Diesel said.

I left Diesel on that note and sashayed off to the bar. It was easy to spot Beaner in the lineup of losers. He was the only one with a raspberry birthmark on his forehead. The stool next to him was unoccupied, so I climbed onto it and made sure there was some air between us.

Beaner was drinking something amber on ice. Probably scotch. I ordered a beer and smiled at him.

"Hi," I said. "How's it going?"

He didn't return the smile. "How much time do you have?" he asked.

"That bad?"

He threw back the liquid in his glass and signaled the bartender for more.

I took another stab at it. "Do you come here often?" I asked him.

"I live here."

"Must be hard to sleep on that barstool. How do you keep from falling off?"

That almost got a smile. "I don't sleep here," he said. "I just drink here. I'd drink at home but that might indicate alcoholism."

"Where's home?"

He made a vague gesture with his hand. "Out there."

"*Out there* is a big place."

"My wife kicked me out of the house," he said. "Changed the locks on the friggin' doors. Married for two hundred years, and she kicked me out of the house. Packed all my clothes in cardboard boxes and put them out on the front lawn."

"Jeez, I'm sorry."

"What am I supposed to do now? Things were different the last time I dated. It was simple back then. You found someone you liked, you asked their father if you could marry them, then you got married and climbed on board." He took possession of his new drink and tested it out. "Don't get me wrong, it's not like I'm saying that was right. It's just the way it was. And I knew that way. Now it's all about talking and sensitivity. I've been married for all this time and suddenly she wants to talk. And it turns out we've been having *bad* sex, and now she wants to have *good* sex. Do you have any idea how embarrassing it is to find out you've been doing it wrong for two hundred years? I mean, how friggin' annoying is that? She said I couldn't find my way south of the border with a road map."

"I might know someone who could help you."

"I don't need help. I need my wife to come to her senses. This whole mess is the result of someone trying to help. Things were fine until some meddler stuck her big fat nose into my marriage. If I get hold of her I'll fix her good. It'll be the last time she meddles in someone's marriage."

"But if she was trying to help—"

"She didn't help. She made things awful." He chugged his drink, dropped a twenty on the bar, and stood. "I've gotta go."

"So soon?"

"Things to do."

"Where are you going? Are you going home?"

My eyes flicked to the bartender when he took the

twenty and the empty glass. A beat later, I turned my attention back to Beaner, but he was gone.

"Where'd he go?" I asked the bartender. "Did you see him leave?"

"I saw him get off the stool, but then he got lost in the crowd."

I left money on the bar and went outside to Diesel.

"He's gone," I said. "We were talking, and he got agitated, and he split."

Diesel was lounging against my car. "I saw him for a second when he walked through the door. A couple people came out with him, and somehow he disappeared behind them before I could get to him." Diesel pushed off from the car, went to the driver's side door, angled himself in behind the wheel, and turned the key in the ignition. "Let's go."

"Wait a minute. This is *my* car. I drive."

"Everybody knows the guy gets to drive."

"Not in Jersey."

"*Especially* in Jersey," Diesel said. "The testosterone level in Jersey is fifteen percent higher than it is in any other state."

4

It was still early, so we stopped at a supermarket on the way home.

"What about the shopping cart?" I asked Diesel. "Do you have to drive that, too?"

"I'd get my nuts repossessed if I didn't drive the shopping cart."

A half hour later, we loaded our food onto the checkout belt, and Diesel gave his credit card to the checker.

"Boy, you've got lots of food," the checker said.

"A man's gotta eat," Diesel told her.

I took a peek at the card. "There's no bank name on this card," I whispered to Diesel.

"It's an Unmentionable card," he said. "Good in three solar systems."

I was pretty sure he was kidding.

I crammed the last of the food into my kitchen . . . lunch meat, beer, cheese, peanut butter, pickles, bagels, ice cream, cereal, milk, orange juice, apples, bananas, bread, cream cheese, coffee, half-and-half, crackers, cookies, chips, salsa, carrots, mixed nuts, and God-knows-what-else.

Diesel took a bag of chips and a beer into the living room and remoted the television on. "This is great," he said. "I can catch the end of the hockey game."

I settled next to him and reached into the chip bag. Bob had been sleeping in the bedroom, but the rustle of a chip bag was a Bob alarm, and in a beat Bob was up and expectantly standing in front of me. I fed him a couple chips, and he flopped down on the floor with his head on my foot.

"Beaner isn't such a bad guy," I said. "He's just frustrated. He's been married for a long time, and all of a sudden his wife isn't satisfied with the status quo. I think Beaner would like to fix things, but he just doesn't know how to get up to speed. He doesn't know how to go about talking to his wife. And he says, according to his wife, he sucks in the sack."

"So give him a pill."

"It's not about *that*. Women don't care about *that*. That's a *man* problem."

"Yeah, I get it," Diesel said. "But a pill would have been easy. This is just plain embarrassing. Maybe I don't have to shut him down. Maybe we can reprogram him."

"We?"

"Unmentionables who've crossed the line aren't happy to see me. And bad things happen when Beaner isn't happy. So either you're going to have to convince him to chill and talk to me, or else you're going to have to get him alone somewhere. I can't seem to follow Beaner, but I can follow you."

"What about his listening-and-understanding problem?"

"I suck at that," Diesel said. "That's girl stuff. You're going to have to explain that to him."

"Only if you help me with Annie Hart's cases. I've scored a big zero with two out of three, and I'm not sure the third one will fly."

Diesel's cell phone buzzed.

"Yeah," Diesel said into the phone. "Now what?"

He slouched deeper into the couch and listened with his mouth set tight. "Yeah," he said. "I hear you. I'm working on it. Send everyone a case of whatever the hell it is they need."

"And?" I said when he disconnected.

"Beaner can't find Annie, so he's visiting her friends and relatives, causing havoc."

The next call was from Annie.

"I'm working on it," Diesel said. "I can't approach him in public and have him contaminate a room filled with innocent people." He nodded and listened. "You have to be patient," he said. "I have a partner. She's helping me with your cases, and she's helping me find Bernie Beaner." More talking on the other end. "No, I'm not bringing her to you. You have to trust me."

Diesel disconnected.

"How'd that go?" I asked him. "Does she trust you?"

"Not even a little. She's coming over here."

"What about Bernie? I thought it wasn't safe for Annie to go out because Bernie might get her."

"She'll get help," Diesel said. "She'll be okay."

I took another handful of chips, fed a couple to Bob, and turned my attention back to the game. A few minutes later, my doorbell rang. Diesel got the door and ushered Annie Hart into my living room. She was a little shorter than me, a little plumper, a little older. She had short, curly brown hair and lively brown eyes and a nice mouth. She smiled at Diesel and me, and the smile produced crinkle lines at the corners of her eyes. She was wearing a bright red hooded jacket, jeans, and boots, and she had her purse tucked into the crook of her arm.

Diesel introduced us. "Annie Hart, this is Stephanie Plum. Stephanie, meet Annie Hart."

I stood and extended my hand. "It's a pleasure."

"Have you seen the files?" she asked me.

"Yes."

"It's very important that you help these people have a good Valentine's Day. And it's so close. Today is Friday and Valentine's Day is Monday. Of course, the real goal is life-long love, but truthfully, that's icing on the cake." She flicked her eyes at Diesel. "We all love Diesel, but relationships aren't his strength. Diesel runs on pure testosterone, and relationships need a little estrogen."

"Pure testosterone . . . that would explain his wardrobe," I said.

Annie and I took a moment to assess the grungy thermal shirt, beat-up boots, and two-day beard.

"Exactly," Annie said. "Although, it seems to work for him."

"You have to go with what you've got," Diesel said.

"I have a good feeling about you," Annie said to me. "You have a lovely aura. I hope you don't mind the intrusion, but I had to see for myself. I really feel much better now. Call me if you have problems. Any time of the day or night. I've made promises to these people, and I hate not to keep a promise. I've really tried hard with Charlene Klinger, but I've been terribly off the mark. She says she doesn't want a man in her life, but I know that's not true. She's a good person, and she deserves to have a loving helpmate."

"Can I get you something?" I asked. "Coffee? A drink?"

"I'd love that, but I promised this would be short. Perhaps when everything is settled we can visit. I know you have some romance problems."

I shot a look at Diesel. "Blabbermouth."

"Oh dear, no," Annie said. "Diesel didn't say anything. I just have a sense of these things. What are you doing on Valentine's Day?"

"No plans so far. I guess Diesel and I will be finishing things up for you."

"My word, you're not going to spend Valentine's Day with Diesel, are you?"

"I hadn't actually thought about it."

"Not a good idea," Annie said. "He's a heartbreaker."

"We don't have that sort of relationship," I told her.

"If you spend enough time in his company, the pheromones will wear you down . . . and the dimples."

"Diesel has dimples?"

"Just ignore them," Annie said. "And don't worry about your issue with commitment. As soon as I get out of jail, we'll have a good sit-down, and I'll solve that problem for you. Goodness, the answer is obvious. Clearly you belong with—"

And Annie was gone.

"Did she just disappear?" I asked Diesel.

Diesel was sunk into the couch. "I don't know. I wasn't watching. I've got hockey on, and the Rangers scored a goal."

"Jeez," I said. "That was weird."

"Yeah, welcome to my world," Diesel said, returning to the bag of chips. "Would you get me another beer?"

I opened my eyes and looked up at Diesel. He was dressed but unshaven, holding a mug of coffee.

"What time is it?" I asked. "And why are you in my bedroom?"

"It's six o'clock. Rise and shine, cutie pie."

"Go away. I'm not ready to rise and shine."

Diesel shoved me over a couple inches, sat on the edge of the bed, and sipped his coffee. "We need to wrap this up before Annie gets restless again."

"What on earth are we going to do at six in the morning?"

"I have plans."

I pushed myself up on my elbow. "You're a real pain in the behind."

"Yeah, people tell me that a lot. You look sexy with your hair all messed, and your eyes kind of sleepy. Maybe I should get under the covers with you."

"What about the early start?"

"This wouldn't take long."

"Easy for you to say. Get out of my bedroom and put an English Muffin in the toaster for me. I'll be out in a minute. And it would help if you'd feed Bob and take him out for a walk."

I took a fast shower, blasted my hair with the hair dryer and pulled it back into a ponytail. I got dressed in a T-shirt and jeans and topped it off with a fleece hoodie.

Diesel was going over Annie Hart's files when I got to the kitchen.

"I fed Bob, and I walked him," Diesel said.

"Did you remember to take a plastic bag for his poop?"

"Sweetheart, I don't do the poop-in-a-bag thing. It's impossible to look like a tough guy when you're carrying a bag of poop. And you might want to think about feeding him less, because apparently whatever goes into a dog comes out of a dog, and it isn't good."

I took my muffin out of the toaster and looked around Diesel's shoulder. He was reading about Charlene Klinger.

"I spoke to her," I told Diesel. "She thinks Annie is a nut, and she doesn't want to get fixed up."

Diesel flipped to Gary Martin.

"He wants our help bad," I said. "Unfortunately, the love of his life is all wrong for him, and I really don't want to stick him with her. He deserves better."

"We're not supposed to change the world," Diesel said. "We're just supposed to set things up for Valentine's Day."

"Valentine's Day isn't going to happen for Gary Martin and Loretta Flack. Flack has maxed out Martin's credit at Tiffany's and moved on to greener pastures."

"That's cold," Diesel said. He turned to Larry Burlew's file. "What about this one?"

"He's got a thing for the girl in the coffee shop across from his butcher shop. I arranged for them to get together, so with any luck he's off the list. I didn't get to the last two cases."

Diesel paged through the rest of the files. "The fourth case is someone named Jeanine Chan. And all it says is she has a problem. Doesn't look like Annie visited her yet. No picture. No case history. And the fifth guy needs help getting married. His name is Albert Kloughn."

I snatched the file out of Diesel's hand. "That's my sister's live-in boyfriend!"

"I remember now," Diesel said. "Last time I was here she found out she was pregnant."

"She had the baby and they had a big wedding planned, and Kloughn had a total panic attack. He broke out in a cold sweat and hyperventilated himself into oblivion. They bailed on the wedding and ran off to Disney World, but he's never been able to bring himself to marry Valerie."

"How about we stun-gun him, and when he wakes up he's married?"

"You're such a romantic."

"I have my moments," Diesel said.

"Now what?"

"Now you put your boots and mittens on, and we go out and do our lame-ass cupid thing."

I shoved my feet into my boots, gathered up my mittens and scarf, and took a moment to call Morelli. Lots of rings. No answer. His answering service came on-line. Morelli was underground, working a sting.

"It's me," I said. "Just wanted to let you know Bob is fine."

Charlene Klinger lived in a narrow single-family, two-story house in North Trenton. It had a postage-stamp yard and a driveway but no garage. A green soccer-mom van was parked in the driveway. A big orange cat sat hunkered down and slitty-eyed on the roof of the van.

Diesel parked my Escape at the curb, and we made our way to the front door. We rang the bell, and Charlene's youngest kid let us in and then instantly disappeared, no questions asked. It was Saturday morning, and the Klinger household was in full chaos mode. The television was on in the living room, a couple of dogs were barking toward the back of the house, rap was blaring from an upstairs bedroom, and Charlene's voice carried from the kitchen.

"You absolutely cannot have ice cream for breakfast," she said. "And don't you dare put it in your orange juice."

I knocked on the doorjamb and looked in at Charlene. "Hi," I said. "Remember me?"

Charlene looked at me open-mouthed. "What are you doing here? How did you get in?"

"A little boy with red hair and a blue shirt let us in," I told her.

"I swear someday we're all gonna get killed in our sleep. He'll open the door to anyone."

"I was hoping I could have just a few minutes to talk to you."

"I've got nothing to say. I don't want a man in my life. I don't have time to talk to you. And—"

Charlene stopped midsentence, and her eyes widened a little when she saw Diesel.

"This is Diesel," I told Charlene. "He's part of the relationship team. He's our, um, man specialist. Are you sure you don't want a man in your life? They can come in handy sometimes . . . taking out the garbage, scaring away burglars, fixing the plumbing."

"I guess," Charlene said. "Is *he* available?"

"Are you?" I asked Diesel.

"Not even a little," Diesel said.

"You wouldn't want him anyway," I told Charlene. "He's

got limitations. I mean, we wouldn't expect Diesel to put a new float in a toilet, right? Plus, I'll bet you'd like a man who could cook sometimes. And Diesel doesn't do that either."

Diesel slid a look at me . . . like maybe he could cook if there was incentive.

"Jeez," Charlene said.

Diesel crossed the kitchen, poured himself a mug of coffee, and slouched against a counter. "There were a bunch of rejected men in your file," he said to Charlene. "Why did you reject them?"

"They rejected *me*. Too many cats. Too many kids. Too old. Too boring."

"So we need to find someone who likes kids," Diesel said. His attention wandered to a cat sleeping on the counter in front of the toaster. "And animals."

"Beyond that, what kind of man do you want?" I asked Charlene.

"Rich?"

"Would you settle for mildly successful?"

"Here's the thing," Charlene said. "I don't want to settle at all. I was serious yesterday when I said I don't have the time or energy for a man right now. I have soup stock cooking on the stove and a week's worth of laundry sitting in the basement next to the washing machine. I have two kids upstairs, listening to rap and figuring out how they can bypass the parental controls on the television. I have a pregnant cat that I know is in the house somewhere but haven't been able to find for two days. My deadbeat ex-husband is learning to surf and living on the beach in Santa Barbara and hasn't sent child support in over a year, so I'm working at the DMV instead of staying home and keeping my kids from turning into juvenile delinquents. I don't need a man. I need a housewife."

"We're counting down to Valentine's Day," I told Charlene. "Let's get the man taken care of first, and then maybe we can work on the housewife."

Charlene turned the flame up under the stockpot. "What would it take to make you go away?"

"A date," Diesel said. "We find you a man, you go out with him, and we leave."

"Is that a promise?" Charlene asked.

"Maybe," Diesel said.

"You have to give us some guidelines," I said to Charlene. "Be honest. What are you really looking for in a man?"

Charlene took a moment. "A *good* man," she said. "Someone who fits with me. Someone comfortable."

The cat got up, stretched on the counter, turned, and attempted to settle itself next to the stove. Its tail flicked into the open flame under the soup stock and instantly caught fire. The cat let out a yowl and jumped from the stove to the table. The black Lab that had been sleeping under the table lunged to its feet and went after the flaming cat.

We were all jumping around, trying to catch the cat, trying to avoid the flaming tail. The Lab slid into a table leg and yelped, Diesel grabbed the cat and dumped a quart of orange juice on him, and I slapped out a burning placemat.

"Hard to believe someone would think you were boring," Diesel said to Charlene.

"Something's wrong with Blackie," the red-haired kid said, looking under the table at the Lab. "He's making whiny sounds and holding his leg funny."

We all looked at Blackie. He was for sure holding his leg funny.

"How bad is the cat?" I asked Diesel.

"Could be worse," Diesel said. "He barbecued the tip of his tail, but the rest of him looks okay. Hard to tell, being that he's soaked in orange juice."

Charlene wrapped a towel around the cat. "Poor kitty."

The twelve-year-old and ten-year-old ran into the kitchen.

"What's happening?" the twelve-year-old asked.

"Kitty set hisself on fire, and Blackie broke his leg," the red-haired kid said.

"Bummer," the twelve-year-old said. And he and his brother turned and went back upstairs. As if this happened every day.

"Where am I going to find a vet at this hour on a Saturday?" Charlene said. "I'm going to have to go to the emergency clinic. It's going to cost me a fortune."

"I know someone who'll help us," I told her. "I have his number in my car."

Charlene cradled the cat close to her and grabbed her

purse off the counter. "Get your coat and hat," she said to the red-haired kid. "And round up your brothers. Everyone out to the van."

Diesel scooped the Lab off the floor and carried him to the door. "Think Blackie could stand to lay off the chow," Diesel said. "This dog weighs a ton."

"He could use a bigger yard," Charlene said. "He never gets to run. He appeared on our front porch in the middle of a snowstorm two years ago and just never left."

The four kids trooped out and got into the van, and I ran to my car for Gary Martin's folder. Diesel locked the house and eased himself into the van with Blackie on his lap, front leg dangling loose. Charlene was in the passenger seat with Kitty still wrapped in the towel. I slid behind the wheel and called Gary Martin on my cell.

"I have an emergency," I told him. "A cat with a barbecued tail and a dog with a broken leg. And I talked to Loretta, but that's a whole other story."

"Is it a sad story?"

"Yeah. The story isn't good."

"My office doesn't open until ten today," Martin said, "but I can come in early. I'll be there in a half hour."

I transferred Bob from the Escape to the rear seat in the soccer-mom van, introduced him to everyone, and took my place behind the wheel.

"Who's the big guy holding Blackie?" the youngest kid asked at the first light.

"His name is Diesel," Charlene said. "Be polite."

"Diesel," the kid repeated. "I never heard of anyone named Diesel."

"Diesel's a train," one of the other kids said.

I adjusted the rearview mirror so I could check Diesel out. Our eyes met and caught for a moment. I couldn't see his mouth, but the little crinkle lines around his eyes told me he was smiling. The Klingers were amusing him.

Lights were on in the clinic when I pulled into the lot. Gary Martin had arrived just in front of us. He still had his coat and hat on when we all swooped in.

"This is Charlene Klinger," I said to Martin. "She's mom to Kitty and Blackie and the four kids."

Charlene introduced the kids. "Junior, Ralph, Ernie, Russell."

Martin looked at Diesel.

"He's with me," I said. "He's the dog-toter."

"I should probably run some film of Blackie's leg, but I don't have an assistant until ten," Martin said.

"I can help," Charlene said. "I've got four kids, three cats, two dogs, a rabbit, and twelve hamsters. I've taped up split lips, delivered kittens, breast-fed four boys, and once we raised chickens from eggs for Ernie's science project."

"The chickens pooped all over the house," Ralph said.

Martin unwrapped the cat enough to look at its tail. "The tail doesn't look too bad," he said. "Mostly he's lost hair, and he's singed the tip. Why is he so sticky?"

"Diesel put the fire out with orange juice," Ralph told him. "It was awesome."

"I need someone to take the cat to the big sink in the back room and very gently wash the orange juice off him," Martin said. "And I need someone to hold Blackie while I run film."

"I can hold Blackie," Russell said. "This is pretty cool. I might want to be a vet someday. I bet you meet a lot of girls."

"I suppose," Martin said. "I'm not exactly the girl expert. I'm better with animals. Animals think I'm cute. Girls just think I'm bald."

"I think you're cute," Charlene said. "You're cuddly . . . like Fluffy."

"Who's Fluffy?" Martin asked.

"Our rabbit," Ralph said. "He weighs a thousand pounds."

"Everything in our house is overweight," Charlene said. "Except the kids."

Martin exchanged his jacket for a blue lab coat. "Maybe I could take a look at Fluffy someday and suggest a better diet."

"It's not just Fluffy," Ralph said. "We practically have a zoo. Mom takes all the rejects."

Gary Martin and Charlene Klinger were perfect for each other. He wanted kids, and she had a pack of them. They were the same age. They were both animal lovers. And he could doctor up Charlene's menagerie when they set themselves on fire. Plus, Charlene Klinger and Gary Martin looked like they belonged together. They were a matched set. Far better than Gary Martin and Loretta What's-Her-Face.

"Do you make house calls?" I asked Martin. "I was thinking it might be better for you to go to Charlene's house to see her animals since she has so many. And since you'd be doing her a favor she could make dinner for you. I bet you hate to eat alone all the time . . . now that you're alone."

"Are you sure I'm alone?" Martin asked.

"Trust me, you're alone."

"I'd love to have you look at my animals," Charlene said, "but I don't know if you want to eat at my house. It gets real hectic at dinnertime."

"I had three sisters and two brothers," Martin said. "I'm good with hectic."

"Can you fix a toilet?" I asked him. "Can you cook?"

"Sure. You don't grow up in a house with three sisters and two brothers and one bathroom and not know something about toilets." Martin took Blackie from Diesel and headed for x-ray. "And I make a killer pork tenderloin. And I can make brownies."

I took Charlene aside. "Did you hear that? He makes brownies."

"What the hell, I shave my legs anyway," Charlene said. "And he reminds me of Fluffy. I guess I could give it a shot. Do you think he's interested?"

"Of course he's interested," I said. "You're a domestic goddess. Just what he wants."

An hour later, Kitty had the end of his tail wrapped in white gauze, and Blackie had a cast on his front leg.

"It was really nice of you to come in early like this," Charlene said to Martin.

"Happy to be able to help," Martin said. "You have great kids. Russell was a terrific assistant."

"Maybe you could come over and check on Blackie and Kitty and Fluffy sometime," Charlene said.

"Sure," Martin said.

We all stood around, waiting. Gary Martin was slow picking up social cues.

After a long moment, Diesel slung an arm around Martin's shoulders. "Maybe you want to check out Charlene's rabbit *tonight*."

The lightbulb went on in Martin's head. "Tonight would be wonderful! I see my last patient at five o'clock, so I could come over around six."

"We're having pot roast tonight if you'd like to take a chance on dinner with us," Charlene said.

"Boy, that would be fantastic. I'll bring dessert. I won't have time to make my brownies, but I'll stop at the bakery."

We got Charlene and her kids and animals back to their house, waved good-bye, and angled ourselves into my car.

Diesel gave me a playful punch in the shoulder. "Are we good, or what?" he said. "Cross two names off our list."

I answered my cell phone.

"Your sister is coming over for dinner tonight," my mother said. "I'm making lasagna, and I've got an ice-cream cake for dessert. I thought you would want to come."

"I think I might be working tonight."

"What, you can't take time out to eat? Everybody has to eat."

"Yes, but I have a partner—"

"There's always extra. Bring your partner. Is it Lula?"

"No."

"Is it Ranger?"

"No."

"Who is it?"

"Diesel."

Silence.

"From that Christmas where our tree burned up?" my mother finally asked.

"Yeah."

I imagined her making the sign of the cross.

"What are you doing with Diesel?" she asked. "No, don't tell me. I don't want to know."

5

It was midmorning and clouds were creeping in above us. We were in front of Jeanine Chan's house, and we were reading her file.

"Not much here," Diesel said. "She's thirty-five. Single. Never been married. No kids. She works at the button factory. File says she has a problem."

Jeanine lived in a single-story, low-rent row house about a quarter mile from my parents' house in the Burg. There were twenty-one units to a block. They were all redbrick. Front doors opened to small stoops that were directly on the sidewalk. Back doors opened to tiny yards that bordered an alley. Two bedrooms, one bath, small eat-in kitchen. No garages. All the units were identical.

I rang the bell twice, the door opened a crack, and Jeanine looked out. "Yes?" she asked.

"We're looking for Jeanine Chan," I said.

"I'm Jeanine."

She was maybe an inch shorter than me. She had brown almond-shaped eyes and shoulder-length dark brown hair.

She was slim and dressed in a gray shapeless sweatshirt and matching sweatpants.

I introduced myself, and then I introduced Diesel.

Jeanine's eyes sort of glazed over when she saw Diesel.

"Annie suggested you might have a problem," I said to Jeanine.

"Who, me?" Jeanine said. "Nope. Not me. Everything's just fine. Hope this wasn't too inconvenient. I have to go now." And she slammed and locked the door.

"That was easy," Diesel said.

"We didn't solve her problem."

"So?"

"So you're paying me to close the deal, and that wasn't closing the deal. Besides, I'm starting to like this match-maker thing. It's a challenge."

I rang the bell again. And again.

"Now what?" Jeanine said, opening the door, sticking her head out.

"I thought you might want to reconsider. Are you sure you don't have a problem?"

Jeanine's eyes locked onto Diesel.

"Excuse me a minute while I confer with my associate," I said to Jeanine.

I took Diesel by the arm and walked him down the sidewalk to the car.

"It's you," I said to Diesel. "You're making her nervous."

"I have that effect on women," Diesel said, smiling. "It's my animal magnetism."

"No doubt. Wait in the car. I'm going to talk to Jeanine, and I'll be right back."

"Okay, what's the problem?" I said to Jeanine when I closed her front door. "I know there's a problem."

"Annie didn't tell you? Gosh, this is so embarrassing. I don't know how to say this." She sucked in some air and scrunched her eyes closed.

"Hello? Anybody home?" I said after a minute of Jeanine with her eyes closed tight.

"I'm working myself up to it," Jeanine said.

"Boy, this must really be bad."

"It's the worst."

"Murder? Cancer? Chocolate allergy?"

Jeanine blew out a sigh. "I can't get laid."

"That's it?"

"Yes."

"That's not so bad," I said. "I think I can handle that. I just have to find a guy to have sex with you?"

"Pretty much."

"Do you have requirements?" I asked her.

"I used to, but I'm getting desperate. I guess I'd like him to have at least *some* teeth. And it would be good if he wasn't so fat he smothered me. That's about it. I got all panicked when I opened the door because I thought maybe Annie sent that Diesel guy over to get the job done. I mean, I wouldn't mind doing it with him, but I might have to work my way up. He doesn't look like something a beginner would want to tackle. Which brings me to the real problem." Jeanine cracked her knuckles. "I'm a virgin."

"Get out!"

"I don't know how this happened. At first I was being careful. I didn't want to do it with just anyone, right? And then all of a sudden I was in my twenties, and it got embarrassing. I mean, how do you explain being twenty-five years old and never once finding a man who was good enough? And the older I got, the worse it became. It turns out virgins are only popular in high school and harems. No one wants to take responsibility for deflowering a thirty-five-year-old woman."

"Jeez, who would have thought?"

"Yeah, knock me over with a feather. I'm telling you, I've really been trying lately, but I can't get anyone to do it. And now, I've found a man I really like. He's funny and he's kind and he's affectionate. I really think this could turn into something. He might even be the love of my life. Problem is, I have to keep finding excuses not to invite him in . . . like, my cat is sick, or my mother is visiting, or there's a gas leak."

"All because you can't tell him you're a virgin?"

"Exactly. He'll run for the hills. They always do! God, I hate this stupid virginity. What a dumb idea, anyway. I mean, how the heck am I supposed to get rid of it?"

"Maybe a doctor could help you."

"I thought of that, but that's only part of it." She cracked her knuckles. "I don't know how to do it. I mean, I know where it goes and all, but I don't know the process. Like, do I just lay there? Or am I supposed to do something?"

"Usually you do what feels good."

"What if it doesn't feel good? I'm thirty-five. I'm old to be starting out. What if it was *use it or lose it*? I need some instruction. Nothing fancy. I'd be happy with the basics. For instance, am I supposed to moan?"

"Men like it, but I find it distracting."

Jeanine was gnawing on her bottom lip. "I don't think I can moan."

"Are you sure you don't want to just talk this out with the guy you're dating?"

"I'd rather stick a fork in my eye."

"Okay, hang in there, and I'll figure something out."

I left Jeanine and trotted back to Diesel.

"You were in there long enough," Diesel said. "What's her big problem?"

"She's a virgin."

"No kidding?"

"Turns out after a certain age it's not that easy to get rid of your virginity. She said men head for the hills when they find out she's a virgin. Don't want the responsibility of being the first."

"I could see that," Diesel said.

"She thought maybe Annie sent you to do the job."

Diesel grinned. "I could take a crack at it."

I raised an eyebrow.

"What?" Diesel said.

"Men."

Diesel grinned wider and ruffled my hair, and I slapped his hand away.

"Just trying to be helpful," Diesel said.

"Jeanine has a boyfriend. She likes him a lot and doesn't want to lose him, but she's afraid he'll split when she tells him she's a virgin."

"So don't tell him," Diesel said. "Let him figure it out for himself after the deed is done."

"That's sort of sneaky."

"You have a problem with sneaky?"

"There's another issue. She feels like she's sort of dumb about the whole thing. Like at thirty-five she should have some technique behind her."

"I imagine you could help her with that one," Diesel said.

"I guess, but I'm not sure I'm all that expert."

"I could test you out and let you know how you score," Diesel said, the grin back in place. "Rate you on a scale of one to ten."

"Now there's an offer every girl dreams about."

Diesel's phone rang, and he took the call.

"Yeah," he said into the phone. "How bad is it?" He listened for a full minute, disconnected, cranked the car over and put it into gear.

"Where are we going?"

"We're going to look for Beaner. He attacked a woman in a diner two blocks from Ernie's Bar. My source said

Beaner went in for breakfast, saw this woman, and went nuts on her because she resembled his wife."

"Jeez. What did he do to her? Is she going to be all right?"

"She'll recover, but it won't be fun." Diesel headed for the center of the city. "I know Beaner is living in the neighborhood around Ernie's. I placed him there a week ago, but I can't get a fix on him. I thought we'd go over and walk around. See if I get a vibe."

I looked back at Bob. "It's freezing. I can't leave Bob sitting in the cold SUV all afternoon."

Diesel hooked a left at the intersection. "We'll drop him off at your apartment. Lock him in your bathroom, so he doesn't eat your couch. Your bathroom is nice and big. He'll be okay."

The neighborhood around Ernie's is a residential and commercial mix. There are office buildings, condo buildings, brownstones, and small businesses like Ernie's Bar all in a jumble. Diesel parked in a lot, and we set out on foot with our collars turned up against the wind and our hands in our pockets to keep warm. We covered a grid of blocks a half-mile square, but Beaner didn't register on Diesel's radar.

We ducked into a deli and got sandwiches and coffee for lunch, happy to be out of the cold.

"This isn't working," I said to Diesel. "I vote we do it my human way and canvass the street, asking questions."

"I'm human," Diesel said. "I just have a few extra skills."

I finished my sandwich and coffee and stood. "You go north and I'll go south, and we'll meet back here at three o'clock."

I started with the girl at the register in the deli, asking if she'd seen a guy with a raspberry birthmark on his face. Her answer was no. I went to the florist next door, the drugstore, the dry cleaner. No one had seen Beaner. I spoke to the doorman at a condo building and the receptionist at a high-rise office building. No Beaner. I went four blocks south, stopping people on the street. I crossed the street and worked my way back to the deli. No luck at all.

By the time I met up with Diesel, wind-driven snow was angling down, stinging my face. Snow is picturesque in Vermont. In New Jersey, it's a pain in the ass. It slows traffic and makes walking treacherous. Dogs turn the snow yellow, and cars churn it into brown sludge.

"Any luck?" Diesel asked.

"None. How about you?"

"Zip."

I felt my cell phone buzz. It was Larry Burlew, and I could barely understand what he was saying. He was talking at warp speed and stuttering.

"It's n-n-not working," he said. "I don't know what to s-s-say to her. She comes over with coffee whenever I wave, but I don't know what to say. What should I say? I just s-s-say *thank you*. I thought I could talk to her, but nothing comes out. I d-d-don't think I can drink much more coffee, but I can't stop myself from waving."

"How many cups have you had?"

"I d-d-don't know. I lost count. Twelve or fifteen, I think."

"We're on our way," I told him. "Try to hang in there, and for God's sake, don't drink any more coffee."

6

Larry Burlew was pacing when we walked into the shop.

"I don't feel good," he said. "I think I'm having a heart attack. My heart is racing. And my eye is twitching. I hate when my eye twitches like this. Maybe I need a cup of coffee to settle my nerves."

"Put a coat on him and walk him around outside in the cold," I told Diesel. "See if you can get some of the caffeine out of his system."

"Who'll take care of the shop?" Burlew asked. "I can't walk out on the shop."

"I'll take care of the shop," I told him. "No one comes in at this time of the day. Don't worry about it."

Five minutes later, a woman walked in and wanted a pork roast deboned and rolled.

"I'm just the assistant butcher," I told her. "I'm not allowed to debone. The real butcher will be back in an hour, but I'm not sure he'll be fit to use sharp tools. How about a nice roasting chicken?"

"I don't want a chicken," she said. "I need a pork roast."

"Okay, how about this. I'll give it to you for free if you'll take it with the bone in. It's a special promotional deal."

"I guess that would be okay," the woman said.

I took a roast out of the display case, wrapped it in white butcher paper, and gave it to the woman.

"Have a nice day," I told her.

Twenty minutes later, Diesel returned with Burlew.

"How's he doing?" I asked Diesel.

"He's stopped stuttering, and his eye has almost completely stopped twitching. I had to bring him back because I think his nose is frostbitten. This weather sucks. I'm putting in for an assignment in the Bahamas after this."

"Can you do that?"

"No. I go where I'm needed. There aren't a lot of people who can do my job."

"Were there any customers?" Burlew asked.

"No," I told him. "Nobody bought anything."

"The coffee delivery scheme isn't working," Diesel said. "We need to think of something else."

"The coffee delivery scheme is perfectly okay. It's Burlew we need to fix. He needs practice," I said. "I'm going to be the coffee person, and you be Larry. I'll walk in, and you start a conversation with me, so he can see how it's done."

I went outside, and then I came in again.

"Here's your coffee," I said to Diesel, pretending to hand him a cup of coffee.

"Thanks," Diesel said. And he grabbed me and kissed me.

I pushed away from him. "What the heck was that about?"

Diesel was rocked back on his heels, smiling. "I felt like kissing you. It was cold outside, and you're all nice and warm."

"Boy. I wish I could do that," Burlew said. "That was great."

"It wasn't great," I said to Burlew. "That was a bad example. Diesel's a nut. I'm going to go out and come in again, and this time I'm going to hand *you* the coffee."

I went outside and stood on the sidewalk for a moment, sucking in cold air. The kiss had actually been pretty damn terrific. Not that it was going to lead to anything, but it was terrific all the same. I pulled myself together and came back in and pretended to hand Burlew a cup of coffee.

Burlew took the coffee and looked at me blank-faced.

"What do you say?" I asked him.

"Thank you."

"What else?"

Burlew was stumped.

"Tell her your name," I said.

"Larry Burlew."

"My name is Jet," I told him.

Silence.

I jumped back in. "Tell her you think her name is unusual. Ask her if it means something."

"That's stupid," Diesel said. "He'll sound like a dork."

"What would you suggest?"

"I'd get right to it. I'd tell her I was going to catch the Knicks game at the sports bar down the street, and I'd ask her if she wanted to join me."

"You can't just say 'Thanks for the coffee' and then ask her out to a bar. It's too abrupt. And how do you know she's a Knicks fan?"

"It doesn't matter. It's a guy thing. It makes him look like a guy. If he says something dorky about her name, she'll think he's a pussy. Anyway, if she wants to go out with him she'll say *yes*. If she doesn't say *yes* you know it's a lost cause and you move on."

"I don't like basketball," Burlew said.

"What do you like?"

"I like opera."

Diesel was hands on hips. "You're shitting me."

Burlew fixed his attention on the display case. "There's a pork roast missing. Are you sure you didn't sell anything?"

"I gave it away. It was a charity thing. Girl Scouts."

Diesel's attention wandered to the street. "Hey, get this," he said. "Coffee Girl must be off work for the day. She's got her coat on, and her purse over her shoulder, and it looks like she's coming over here. She's out of the coffee shop and crossing the street."

"Oh no," Burlew said. "She doesn't have more coffee, does she?"

"No," Diesel said. "No coffee."

The bell chimed on the front door, and Jet walked in. "Hi," she said to me. "Your cousin is going to make me employee of the month for selling so much coffee." Her attention turned to Diesel. "*Hello,*" she said.

"He's gay," I told her. "Flaming."

Jet sighed. "I knew he was too good to be true." She looked over at Larry Burlew.

"Straight as an arrow," I said.

Jet nodded. "It's important to know stuff like that about your . . . butcher. Like, is he married?"

"Nope. Totally available."

"So I would be smart to buy meat here?"

"You wouldn't regret it," I said.

"Good. I feel like steak tonight."

Diesel slid a look at me. "Carnivore," he whispered.

Jet directed her attention to Burlew. "What looks tasty?"

"Do you want to grill it, or broil it, or pan-fry it?" Burlew asked.

"I don't know. Something healthy."

"I have a great recipe that I do with sirloin," Burlew said. "I marinate it and then I broil it with vegetables."

"That sounds terrific," Jet said. "Maybe you could show me how to do it."

"Sure," Burlew said. "It's real easy. I could do it tonight if you want. And I'll bring the steak and stuff with me."

Jet wrote her address on a scrap of butcher paper. "Come over whenever you're done with work. I'll get some wine." And she left.

Diesel and I looked at Burlew.

"What the hell was that?" Diesel asked.

"I'm good when it comes to meat," Burlew said.

It was twilight when we left the butcher shop. Streetlights were glowing behind swirling snow, and Trenton was looking cold but cozy.

"We're hot at this relationship shit," Diesel said. "We do things all wrong, and it all turns out right."

We drove back to Beaner's neighborhood and cruised several blocks. Diesel stopped in front of Ernie's, and I ran in to take a fast look. No Beaner in sight, so I returned to the car.

"It's too early," Diesel said. "We should come back around eight."

"We need to get to my parents' house anyway," I told him. "I said we'd be there for dinner."

"We?"

"I didn't want you to feel left out."

"I remember your parents. They run a loony bin."

"Okay. Fine. Drop me off at the door."

"No way," Diesel said. "I wouldn't miss this for anything."

"We just have to make a fast stop at my apartment to get Bob."

A half hour later, we opened my bathroom door, and Bob looked out at us, all droopy-eyed and drooling and panting.

He did some pathetic whimpering noises, opened his mouth, and said *gak*! And barfed up a roll of toilet paper.

"Better than a couch," Diesel said.

I cleaned up the toilet paper and put a new roll in the holder. By the time I was done, Bob was completely perked up, affectionately rubbing against Diesel, spreading dog slime the length of his leg.

"Probably I should change clothes before we go to your parents' house," Diesel said.

For sure.

Diesel pulled a pair of jeans and a shirt out of his backpack. They were exact duplicates of what he was wearing, minus the slime and pizza sauce. No better, no worse. He peeled his shirt off, unlaced his boots, and stepped out of his boots and jeans.

"Good God," I said and whirled around, so I wasn't facing him. Not that it mattered. The image of Diesel in briefs was burned into my brain. Ranger and Morelli, the two men in my life, were physically perfect in very different ways.

Ranger was Cuban American with dark skin and dark eyes and sometimes dark intentions. He had a kickboxer's body and Special Forces skills. Morelli was hard and angular, his temperament Italian, his muscle and skill acquired on the street. Diesel was put together on a larger scale. And while I couldn't see details, I suspected he was larger *everywhere*.

My grandmother was setting the table when we arrived. The extension was in, and the kitchen chairs and a kid's high chair had been brought out to seat ten. Valerie and Albert were already there. Albert was watching television with my dad. I could hear Valerie in the kitchen talking to my mom. Her oldest girl, Angie, was on the floor in the living room coloring in a coloring book. The middle kid, Mary Alice, was galloping around the dining room table, pretending she was a horse. The baby was on Albert's lap.

All action stopped when Diesel walked in.

"Oh jeez," my father said.

"Nice to see you again, sir," Diesel said.

"I remember you," Mary Alice said. "You used to have a ponytail."

"I did," Diesel said, "but I thought it was time for a change."

"Sometimes I'm a reindeer," Mary Alice said.

"Is it different from being a horse?" Diesel asked her.

"Yeah, 'cause when I'm a reindeer I got antlers, and I can fly like Rudolph."

"Can not," Angie said.

"Can, too."

"Can not."

"I can fly a little," Mary Alice said.

I cut my eyes to Diesel.

Diesel smiled and shrugged.

I let Bob off his leash, left Diesel in the living room to

charm my father, and went to the kitchen to check in with my mother. "Is there anything I can do?" I asked.

"You can spoon the red sauce into the gravy boat, and you can try to talk some sense into your grandmother. She won't listen to me."

"Now what?"

"Have you seen her?"

"She was setting the table."

"Did you take a good look?"

Grandma Mazur shuffled into the kitchen. She was in her seventies, and gravity hadn't been kind. She was all slack skin and dimpled flesh draped on a wiry frame. Her hair was steel gray and permed. Her teeth were bought. Her eyes didn't miss much. Her lips were horribly swollen.

"We're oud a nakins," she said. "There's no ore in da china canet."

"Omigod," I said. "What happened to your mouth?"

"Sexy, hunh?" Grandma said.

"She had her lips plumped up," my mother said. "She went to some idiot doctor and had herself injected."

"An nex eek I'n gettin' ass inlans," Grandma said. "No ore saggy ass for ee."

"Ass implants are serious," I told her. "You might not want to do that."

"Ere's a sale on inlans nex eek," Grandma said. "I hade ta niss a sale."

"Yes, but implants have to be incredibly painful. You won't be able to sit. Why don't we just find a sale on shoes?

We can go to Macy's and then have lunch in the food court."

"Okay," Grandma said. "At sounds like un."

My mother took the lasagna and I took the red sauce and Grandma took a basket of bread to the table. Everyone seated themselves and dug in.

Grandma Mazur took some lasagna and poured herself a glass of red wine. She forked some lasagna into her mouth and took a sip of wine and everything fell out of her mouth, onto her lap.

Bob rushed over and ate the food off Grandma's lap, and then settled himself back under the table, ever alert.

"Ny lith are oo ig," she said. "Dey don ork."

My mother jumped up and returned with a straw for Grandma and a tumbler of booze for herself.

My father had his head bent over his lasagna. "Just shoot me," he said.

"I like lasagna," Albert Kloughn said. "It stays on your plate. And if you don't use too much red sauce, hardly any gets on your shirt."

Kloughn was a struggling lawyer who got his degree from the Acme School of Law in Barbados. He was a nice guy, but he was as soft as a fresh nuked dinner roll, and his upper lip broke out into a sweat when he got nervous . . . which was a lot.

"How's the law business?" I asked him.

"It's good. I even have a couple clients. Okay, one eventually died, but that happens sometimes, right?"

"And how's the new house?"

"It's working out real good. It's a lot better than living with my mother."

"And what about getting married?"

Kloughn turned white, farted, and fell off his chair in a faint.

Diesel got up and dragged Kloughn to his feet and sat him back in his chair. "Take a deep breath," Diesel said to Kloughn.

"How embarrassing," Kloughn said.

"Dude," Diesel said, "everyone feels like that about marriage. Get over it."

"Poor snuggle uggums," Valerie said, spoon-feeding Kloughn some noodles. "Did him hurt himself?"

Diesel draped an arm across my shoulders and put his mouth to my ear. "We definitely want to go with the stun gun. In fact, I think we should stun-gun *both* of them."

"Maybe you can get Albert to take a walk with you after dinner, and you can talk to him. He got in touch with Annie and asked for help, so he's obviously motivated."

"That would be high on the list of things I don't want to do. Second only to getting zapped by Beaner."

"About Beaner . . . just exactly what is it that happens when he zaps someone?"

"You don't want to know. And I don't want to tell you. Let's just leave it alone for now."

"I've been thinking about Beaner. Maybe we should talk to *Mrs.* Beaner. Does she live in the Trenton area?"

"She lives in Hamilton Township."

"Is she Unmentionable? Does she have scary, evil skills?"

"She's mildly Unmentionable. Doesn't do much with it. Mostly parlor tricks. Bending spoons and winning at rummy. I interviewed her when I got the Beaner assignment."

"And?"

"You know everything I know. She said she was tired of marriage. Wanted to try something else. She told me Beaner blamed it all on Annie Hart, but Annie didn't have anything to do with it. Annie was just a friend. She didn't know where Beaner was staying, but clearly it was in the Trenton area because he was determined to get even with Annie."

"That's it? Why didn't you ask her to lure Beaner over to discuss things, and then you could jump out of the closet and do your bounty hunter thing and capture Beaner?"

"She knows better than to be around when Beaner goes down. There'll be fallout, and she wants no part of it."

"What about you? Aren't you afraid of Beaner?"

"It takes a lot to damage me, and Beaner doesn't have that kind of power. The best he could do is make me mildly uncomfortable."

"Okay, how about this? We get Mrs. Beaner to lie to her husband. Set up a bogus meeting."

"Tried that. She wouldn't do it."

I mushed a piece of bread around in my leftover sauce. "You know what *that* means."

Diesel did a palms-up. He didn't know what it meant.

"She still cares about him," I said. "She doesn't want to betray him. She doesn't want him captured and neutralized or whatever it is that you do."

Diesel helped himself to a second chunk of lasagna. "Maybe. Or maybe she just doesn't want to get involved."

"I could talk to her."

"Probably not a bad idea," Diesel said. He looked at his watch. "Here's the plan. I get Albert out into the air and walk him around the block and try to figure out what the heck he wants to do about getting married. You talk to your sister and see if she's on board. And at eight, we try our luck at Ernie's Bar. If thing's don't work out, tomorrow you visit Mrs. Beaner."

7

We were in my car, on our way to Ernie's. It had stopped snowing, but the sky was moonless black, and the air had a bite to it.

"How'd it go with Albert?" I asked Diesel.

"He didn't faint, but he wasn't real coherent. From what I can tell, he wants to get married, but the thought of the ceremony freaks him out. Apparently the poor guy's even tried getting hypnotized, but he still can't get down the aisle."

"How about tranquilizers?"

"He said he tried them and had an allergic reaction and went gonzo."

"I talked to Valerie, and she pretty much told me the same thing. Not that I didn't know it already. He's really a sweet guy. He loves the kids, and he loves Valerie, and I know he would love *being* married. It's *getting* married that's the problem."

Diesel cruised down the street and pulled to the curb across from Ernie's.

"Is he in there?" I asked Diesel.

"I don't think so," Diesel said after a couple beats, "but it wouldn't hurt for you to take a look anyway."

I crossed the street, pushed through the big oak door into the warm pub, and hiked myself up onto a barstool. No trouble claiming a seat. Ernie's was an after-work place, not a Saturday night date destination, and it was eerily empty. A few regulars nursed drinks at the bar and numbly watched the overhead television. The tables were empty. The lone bartender ambled over to me.

"What'll it be?" he asked.

"I'm looking for a friend. He was here last night. Has a birthmark on his face. His name's Bernie."

"Yeah, I know the guy. Didn't know his name was Bernie. Not real talky. Pays in cash. He hasn't been in today. We get a different crowd during the week. Saturday and Sunday it's real slow. Were you supposed to meet him?"

"No. Just thought I might run into him."

I left the bar and returned to the car. "He's not there," I told Diesel. "The bartender said he hasn't seen him. Maybe we spooked him off this afternoon. Maybe he saw us walking around looking for him."

Diesel was behind the wheel with his phone in his hand. "I have a problem," he said. "Annie isn't answering. I check on her four times a day. This is the first time she hasn't answered."

"Maybe she's in the shower."

"She knows I call at this time. She's supposed to be

there. I'm having a guy I know drop in on her. He lives in her building."

"Why aren't you staying with him?"

"He has a girl living with him. And he'd drive me nuts. You drive me nuts, too, but in a more interesting way."

Oh boy. "Do you think Beaner found Annie?"

Diesel did a palms-up. "Don't know."

Diesel's phone rang, and he looked at the readout. "It's Flash," he said to me.

"The guy in Annie's building?"

"Yeah."

A minute later, Diesel disconnected, put the car in gear, and pulled into the stream of traffic. "She isn't in the apartment. The door was locked. Nothing seemed to be disturbed."

"Did she take her purse?" I asked him.

Diesel looked at me blank-faced. "Don't know."

"Boots? Coat?"

"Don't know."

"Were the lights left on?"

"Don't know." He hung a U-turn and headed for the center of the city. "Let's go take a look."

Twenty minutes later, we were on a side street in downtown Trenton. Diesel used a passkey to get into an underground garage, parked the car, and we took the elevator to the seventh floor, leaving Bob in the car. There were four apartments on the floor. Diesel knocked on 704 and unlocked the door. We stepped inside and looked around.

Lights were on. There was a purse on the kitchen counter. Wallet and assorted junk inside the purse. No keys. I checked closets. No winter coat or jacket. No boots.

"Here's what I think," I said to Diesel. "She took her keys and winter coat, but she left her purse behind. So I think she stepped out for a moment and didn't intend to go far. Maybe she just needed air or wanted to walk a little. And then maybe something unexpected happened to her."

It was a nice apartment. Not fancy, but tastefully decorated and comfortable. Small kitchen, living room, dining alcove, single bedroom, and bath.

"It's a pleasant apartment," I said to Diesel, "but I can see where Annie would get squirrelly after being cooped up here for a few days. Her phone wasn't in her purse. Why don't you try calling her phone again?"

Diesel dialed Annie on his cell. After a couple beats, we heard the phone ringing. We followed the sound to the bedroom and found her cell phone on the floor by the bed.

"I don't know what to think," I said to Diesel. "I take my phone everywhere with me. I don't know why she'd leave her phone here, except that it's on the floor so maybe it fell out of her pocket."

Diesel wrote a note on a sticky pad in the kitchen and pasted the note to the refrigerator. The message was simple. CALL ME IMMEDIATELY.

We locked up behind ourselves and took the elevator to

the garage. We drove out to the street, and I had a genius idea. We were only two blocks away from the Pleasure Treasure. It was open until ten on Saturdays, and it probably had a book Jeanine-the-Virgin would find helpful.

"Turn right at the next corner," I told Diesel. "There's a sex-toys store two blocks from here, and we might be able to find a book for Jeanine."

I could see Diesel smile in the dark car. "Just when I think my day's in the toilet you suggest a sex-toys store. Honey, you're a ray of sunshine."

"I hate to rain on your parade, but I know about this place because I made a bust here in the fall."

"Then let's hope this trip is more fun, because I could really use some fun."

Diesel parked in the small lot next to the store. I promised Bob a bedtime snack if he'd be a good dog just a little longer, and Diesel and I went inside. We were the only shoppers. A solitary clerk was behind the counter reading a movie star magazine. She looked up when we entered and sucked in some air when she saw Diesel. She was in her twenties and completely punked-out with black-rimmed eyes and multiple piercings.

"Just browsing," I told her.

"Sure," she said. "Let me know if I can help."

Diesel followed me to the book section, selected a book, and thumbed through.

"Is it good?" I asked.

"Yeah, look at this," Diesel said. "Have you ever tried this?"

I looked at the picture. "That's got to be uncomfortable, if not impossible."

"Hey, pictures don't lie. They're doing it." He draped an arm around me and put his mouth to my ear. "I bet I could do it."

"You're a sick man. Maybe we should ask Raccoon Woman if she has a starter book. If we show this to Jeanine, she's liable to check herself into a nunnery."

Diesel pulled another book off the shelf. "This looks more basic. It starts off with anatomy. And there are photographs . . . of everything. We should buy two of these."

It was sort of embarrassing to be looking at crotch shots with Diesel. "Sure," I said, "buy two." I glanced at my watch. "Jeez, look at the time. If we hurry we can catch the end of the game."

"What game is that?" Diesel wanted to know.

"I don't know. Any game."

Diesel moved to the video section. "We should get Jeanine a movie. They've got some good ones."

"No. No movies for Jeanine. Jeanine isn't into moaning, and they always do a lot of moaning in the movies."

"Moaning is fun," Diesel said.

I cut my eyes to him. "Do you moan?"

"Not usually."

"Why not?"

"I'd feel stupid."

"Exactly. Just pay for the books with your phony credit card and let's go home."

"Bet I could make *you* moan," Diesel said, smiling.

"I feel like moaning now," I told him. "And it has nothing to do with sex."

I unwrapped my scarf and hung it on a hook on the wall next to my front door. I draped my heavy winter jacket over the scarf and exchanged my snow boots for shearling slippers.

"I can't believe you bought all that stuff," I said to Diesel.

"It's for Jeanine . . . unless you want to take something for a test drive."

"No."

"Are you sure? We've got a bag full of fun here. I bet we've got samples of every condom ever invented."

"No!"

Diesel set the bag on the kitchen counter and went to the refrigerator. He backed out with a couple beers. "You know what your problem is? You're too uptight."

"I'm not uptight. I've got a boyfriend, and I don't mess around."

"Admirable, but this living arrangement would work better if you had fewer scruples," Diesel said. "I don't fit on the couch."

"Do you fit on the floor?"

"That's cruel," Diesel said.

I took a beer from him and unwrapped a loaf of bread

that had been sitting on the counter. We made a stack of peanut butter sandwiches, gave one to Bob, and took the beer and the rest of the sandwiches into the living room and turned the television on.

"I want to know about Beaner," I said to Diesel. "What are his powers? What kind of chaos does he cause?"

"I'd like to tell you, but then I'd have to kill you. . . ."

"Tell me anyway."

"I'd really rather not."

"Great. Don't tell me. I'll get the story from Mrs. Beaner tomorrow."

"Okay, I'll tell you," Diesel said, "but if you laugh, I swear I'll turn you into a toad."

"You can't actually do that, can you?"

"The better question is, *would I*? And the answer is, *no*."

"About Beaner."

Diesel washed a sandwich down with half a beer. "He can give you a rash."

"A rash?"

"Yep."

"That's it?"

"Sweetie pie, this isn't any ordinary rash. It's the mother of all rashes. It makes you itch *everywhere*. It's nonstop torture for anywhere from three days to three weeks. It's related to poison sumac and looks like hives. Doesn't necessarily leave scars unless you start carving yourself up with a knife because you can't stand the itching."

"Wow."

Diesel sunk low into the couch and closed his eyes. "Who am I trying to kid? It's a rash, for crying out loud. How bad can a rash be?" He pressed the heels of his hands into his eyes. "Used to be I tracked dangerous sexual deviants and insane despots. Last time I was here I disabled a guy who shut down the northeast power grid at Christmas. That's the kind of stuff you can get your teeth into." He sunk lower and groaned. "And now I'm hunting Mr. Itchy. Do you have any idea what this does for my image?"

"It's not good?"

"It's a nightmare. There's no way to even put a decent spin on it. Big bad Diesel is out to shut down a poor slob whose only claim to fame is his ability to give people hives."

I burst out laughing. "I like it."

I went to the kitchen and brought a bag of cookies back to Diesel. I opened the bag, and we each took a cookie and Bob got two.

"How does he do it?" I asked Diesel. "Is this some kind of contact skin disease?"

"I don't know how he does it. I've never actually seen it happen firsthand, but I know he can spread the rash without contact."

"Maybe Beaner would give Annie a rash, and be done with it. Maybe he just needs to get it out of his system," I said to Diesel.

Diesel shook his head. "He's nutso. He was stalking her, reinfecting her every chance he got. It was ugly. Annie had hives on top of hives."

"Tell me more about Beaner."

"He has some minor skills. He's good with mechanical things. Used to own a garage. Sold it last year and is sort of retired. Probably was driving his wife nuts hanging around the house. He's pretty much a normal guy with the exception of this rash thing. And until a week ago, it was completely undercover. People would break out in unexplained hives, and that was the end of it. When his wife left, and he decided Annie was responsible, he went public. For the first couple days it was just directed at Annie, but then he lost control and started lashing out at random people whenever he got angry."

"Bummer."

"Yeah, big whoopitydo. Anyway, I was told to shut him down."

"You don't mean *shut him down* as in . . . permanently?"

"*Shut him down* as in pull the plug on his power."

"You can do that?"

"I have ways."

I was curious about those ways, but I didn't think he'd tell me. And probably it was better not to know, so I ate two more cookies and shoved off the couch. "I'm going to bed. See you in the morning."

I woke up to the sun shining through the vertical crack in my bedroom curtain and a heavy arm draped across my chest. Diesel was sprawled next to me, looking more disreputable than ever with a four-day-old beard. Like I don't have enough problems with the men in my life, now I have a third guy crawling into my bed. Too much of a good thing. At least I was still wearing my pajamas. That was comforting.

I eased away from Diesel, slithered from under the arm, and rolled out of bed. I grabbed some clean clothes, locked myself in the bathroom, and hopped into the shower. I had a full day ahead of me. Talk to Mrs. Beaner and check on Gary Martin, Charlene Klinger, and Larry Burlew. I had the Pleasure Treasure bag to take to Jeanine. And then there was Annie Hart. I was hoping Annie was back in her apartment, but I thought it was unlikely.

By the time I emerged from the bathroom, Diesel was out of bed, standing at my kitchen counter, eating a bowl of cereal.

"I fed and walked the dog," Diesel said. "I didn't know what to do about the rat."

"Hamster."

"Whatever."

I gave Rex fresh water, filled his bowl with hamster crunchies, and poured out some cereal for myself. "Have you heard from Annie?" I asked Diesel.

"No. She didn't answer when I called this morning, so I had Flash check on her apartment again. Still empty." He put his cereal bowl in the dishwasher. "I need to go solo this morning and try to get a fix on Annie. I'm going to jump in the shower and take off. I wrote Beaner's wife's address on the pad on the counter. Her name is Betty. She's expecting you. I don't know how helpful she'll be, but you can give it a shot. I'll be on my cell. The number's also on the pad."

"Do you have a car?"

"I can get one."

Okay, I wasn't going to ask questions about that either.

I was standing at the counter, enjoying a second cup of coffee, when Diesel walked into the kitchen. His hair was still damp, and he smelled like my shower gel. He had his jacket on, and his scarf wound around his neck. "Catch up with you later," he said.

I blinked, and he was gone. Not magically. Out the door, down the hall, to the elevator.

I rinsed my cup and went to the bathroom to brush my teeth. I turned to leave the bathroom and bumped into Ranger. I shrieked and jumped away.

"Didn't mean to startle you," he said.

Usually I sense Ranger behind me by the change in air pressure and the hint of desire. I wasn't paying attention today, and I was caught by surprise.

"Men keep sneaking up on me," I told him.

"I saw Diesel leave."

"Do you know Diesel?"

"From a distance," Ranger said. "Is Diesel a problem?"

"No more than usual. We're sort of working together."

"I have to go out of town for a couple days. Tank will be

here. And I'll be on my cell. I need to talk to you when I get back." He brushed a light kiss across my lips and left.

"The man of mystery," I said to the closed door.

"I heard that," Ranger said from the other side.

8

I dropped Bob at my parents' house and asked them to dog-sit. I had coffee with my mother and Grandma, and by the time I rolled down Betty Beaner's street, it was a little past nine. I parked in her driveway and checked out her house. Average suburbia in every way. Two-story colonial. Landscaped front yard. Fenced back yard. Two-car garage. Freshly painted.

I rang the bell, and Betty answered on the second ring. She was shorter than me and pleasantly round. She had a round face with a nice mouth that looked like it smiled a lot, round wide-open eyes, rounded hips, and big round breasts. She was a Rubenesque woman. She looked to be around fifty.

I extended my hand. "Stephanie Plum."

"I've been expecting you," she said. "Diesel called."

"We thought you might be able to help us with Bernie."

"I can't believe he's running around giving out hives like a senile old fool. I swear, the man is an embarrassment."

I followed her through the living room and dining room

and into the kitchen. She'd been at the small kitchen table, reading the paper, drinking coffee. It was a charming room decorated in warm tones. Rusts and yellows mostly. Small-print wallpaper and matching curtains on the windows.

Betty poured a cup of coffee out for me, and we sat at the table. I looked down at the paper and realized she'd been looking at the want ads.

"Getting a job?" I asked her.

Betty had a red pen on the table by the paper, but none of the ads were circled. "I've been thinking about it. Problem is, I can't do anything. I've been a housewife all these years."

"Two hundred?"

She smiled. "Yes. At least, it seems like that. Actually, Bernie and I have been married for thirty-five years. He was working in a garage, and I took my car in there to get fixed, and next thing we were married."

I sipped my coffee, and I looked at Betty Beaner. She didn't seem angry when she spoke of Bernie. If anything, there was affection. And tolerance. In fact, she reminded me of my mom. My parents didn't have the perfect marriage, but over the years they'd developed a plan to make things work. My mother made my dad feel like he was king of the castle, and my dad abdicated the kingdom over to my mom.

"I know I'm going to sound nosey," I said, "but I haven't got a lot of time, and I'm trying to help Diesel fix things. What went wrong?"

"Snoring."

"That's it? That's the whole thing?"

"Have you ever tried to sleep with a man who snores?"

"No. The men in my life don't snore."

"Bernie didn't used to snore and then one day there it was . . . he was a snorer."

"Aren't there things you can do about snoring?"

"He refuses to believe he snores. He says I'm making a big thing of it, but he wakes me up all night long. I'm always tired. And if I go sleep in the guest room, he gets mad. He says married people should sleep together. So, the hell with him, I'm filing for divorce."

"He thinks this is about talking and sex."

"Of course it's about talking. Talking about snoring! It's not like I wanted to have big touchy-feely discussions with Bernie. It's not like I asked him to join a book group or something. I just wanted him to listen to me. When I say I can't sleep, I mean *I can't sleep*!"

"And what about the sex?"

"I threw that in as a bonus. I figured, what the heck, if I was going to complain I might as well do it right."

Betty circled an ad in the paper with the red pen. "Here's one I bet I could do. They're looking for tollbooth money collectors on the Turnpike."

"Have you thought about counseling?"

"Are you kidding? Do you think a man who won't admit to snoring is going to sign up for counseling? I even tried recording him. He said it was a trick. He said it for sure wasn't him."

"If I could get Bernie to admit to snoring, would you take him back?"

"I don't know. I'm getting used to being alone. The house is nice and quiet. And I get to watch whatever I want on television. Of course, it was a real pain to have to shovel the walk when it snowed."

"This looks like a three-bedroom house. Suppose I could get you your own room with your own television for those nights when Bernie snores? And suppose I could throw in better sex? I don't know firsthand, but I suspect Diesel knows what he's doing. I could get him to talk to Bernie."

This got both of us smiling. Diesel and Bernie discussing sex. Worth the price of a ticket right there.

I decided to take the Pleasure Treasure bag to Jeanine while I was in sex-help mode, so I called and told her I was on my way over.

"Thank goodness," Jeanine said. "I have a date tonight. I was afraid I was going to have to fake an appendicitis attack."

Twenty minutes later, I was at her door.

"Here it is," I said, shoving the bag at her. "Everything you need to know about sex . . . I think."

Jeanine looked inside. "What is all this?"

"You've got a beginner's-guide-to-sex book. And a video that I've never actually seen but Diesel thought looked hot. And then there are some oils. Directions are included. Assorted condoms. And the salesclerk threw in a vibrating penis as a bonus."

Jeanine pulled the penis out of the bag. "Eeeuuw."

I agreed. It wasn't the most attractive penis I'd ever seen. But then maybe it wasn't a fair comparison because lately I'd seen some top-of-the-line equipment.

"It was free," I said by way of apology.

Jeanine paged through the book. "This looks helpful. I always wanted to buy a book like this but could never get up the nerve."

"I thought you could read the book, and then if you have questions you can call me, and I'll try to answer them."

"Maybe I should start with the movie," she said. "Do you want to watch it with me?"

"Think I'll pass. My experience with these movies is that they're made for men and mostly show a lot of boob."

"That would be disappointing," Jeanine said. "I can see that in the locker room at the gym." She peeled a sticky strip off the front cover and gasped. "Holy cow."

I looked over her shoulder. "Double holy cow."

"It's a man," Jeanine said. "And he's naked. I haven't seen a lot of men, so I'm no expert, but I didn't think they came this big."

I took a closer look. "They must have used Photoshop. This is a horse wanger."

"It says on the cover that it's all real and nothing's been retouched."

I took my jacket off. "I guess I could spare a few minutes to make sure everything's authentic. Wouldn't want you getting wrong information. Go ahead and pop that bad boy into the DVD player."

"It's eleven o'clock," Jeanine said. "Almost lunchtime. Maybe we need a glass of wine to get through this."

I agreed. This had all the earmarks of a movie that required booze.

Twenty minutes later, we were sipping wine and leaning forward, eyes glued to the screen.

"This is a car crash," I said. "One of the worst movies ever made. And I can't tear myself away from it."

"Yeah," Jeanine said. "I might have to watch it again just to make sure I've got it all straight."

The doorbell rang, and we both jumped.

Jeanine squeezed her eyes shut. "Please God, don't let it be my mother."

"Does your mother live in the Burg?"

Jeanine hit the pause button. "She lives in Milwaukee."

"So chances are good it's not your mother."

"It was a gut reaction."

Jeanine opened the door, and Grandma leaned to the side to see around Jeanine. She spotted me on the couch and gave a little finger wave.

"I knew that was your car out front," Grandma said. "I'm on my way to the funeral home now that my lips have deflated enough so I can talk. Elaine Gracey is being laid out for a special noon viewing. Your father's off to the lodge with the car, so I had to walk and I'm about froze." She gaped at the television screen where Big Chief and Vanessa Dickbender were frozen in full rut. "I bet you're watching cable," Grandma said. "These reality shows just keep getting better and better. I wouldn't mind sitting down to watch some. Just until I get warmed up. Are you drinking wine? A glass of wine would be real nice."

I heard a car door slam outside, and moments later Jeanine's bell rang again. Jeanine opened the door, and Lula looked in at us.

"I was driving by on my way back from church, and I saw the car and I thought I saw Grandma come in here," Lula said. "Are you guys having a party? Dang, whose hairy ass is that on your television screen?"

"Big Chief," Jeanine said.

"He's the best," Lula said, taking her coat off, pushing in next to Grandma on the couch. "Are we having wine?"

Jeanine brought two more glasses and the bottle, and I hit the PLAY button.

"Now see this here," Lula said, watching Dickbender work over Big Chief. "I've done this lots of times, and she's doing it all wrong."

"Lula was a professional," Grandma told Jeanine. "She was the best on her corner."

"Darn right," Lula said. "I knew what I was doing."

Jeanine filled Lula's glass with wine. "Maybe you could give me some pointers."

"Sure," Lula said. "I'm retired now, so I can share my secrets to being a successful 'ho. The thing is, you gotta get a good rhythm going. My signature move was to do it to 'Jingle Bells.' Everybody loves 'Jingle Bells.' " Lula beat out the rhythm on the coffee table. "Jingle bells. Jingle bells. Jingle *all* the *way* . . . unh!"

"Boy," Jeanine said, "this is just what I need to know."

"Yep," Lula said, "you just keep singing 'Jingle Bells,' and before you know it you can collect your fifteen dollars and leave."

"I could do that," Grandma said. "I can sing 'Jingle Bells,' and I could use an extra fifteen dollars."

Vanessa Dickbender let out a shriek, and we all sucked in some air.

"What was that?" Jeanine wanted to know. "What happened?"

"That might have been a orgasm," Lula said.

"Yikes," Jeanine said. "It sounded painful."

Lula sat back. "Yeah, it was probably fake, but I guess it was supposed to be a big one."

Jeanine poured herself another glass of wine.

"I think he's getting to the end," Lula said. "I can tell on account of all the veins have popped out in Big Chief's face, and he looks like he's gonna have a heart attack. How long's he been doing this anyway?"

"It's been going on for about forty minutes now," I told her.

"Nobody got staying power like Big Chief," Lula said. "He did it in the back of a car one time for ninety minutes. The film is a classic. And I hear they had to hook him up to one of them IV fluid bags when he was done."

"This is kind of scary," Jeanine said. "Maybe I should learn CPR."

"It won't be scary," I said to Jeanine. "You'll be fine. Just keep singing 'Jingle Bells.' "

It was early afternoon when I dropped Grandma off at my parents' house.

"Sorry you missed the viewing," I told her.

"That's okay," she said. "It's not every day I get to see a real good educational film. And I'll get another crack at Elaine tonight."

I watched to make sure Grandma got inside, and then I took off. I drove two blocks, and my cell phone rang.

"I'm right behind you," Diesel said. "Pull over and park. I want to talk to you."

I parked at the curb and got out of my car. Diesel did the same. He was driving a shiny black Corvette that was in direct contrast to all the other salt-and-grime-encrusted cars on the road.

"Nice car," I said. "Clean."

"How'd it go with Betty Beaner?"

"Turns out Bernie snores."

"And?"

"Betty can't sleep. She wants her own room, so she can sleep."

"That's it?"

"She wants a television in the room. And she wants better sex."

"Honey, we *all* want better sex."

I raised an eyebrow.

"What?" Diesel said.

"Someone needs to talk to Bernie."

"Not me."

"I thought you were the big sex hotshot."

"I do okay, but I'm not giving Bernie a birds and bees talk. Guys don't do that. It's . . . weird."

"Yes, but you're an Unmentionable guy."

Diesel had his thumbs hooked into his jeans pockets, and his face set on *don't mess with me.*

"Fine," I said to him. "Have it your way. Don't talk to poor Bernie. Go shut him down."

"I don't believe this," Diesel said. "It just gets worse and worse. Bad enough I have to play cupid to a butcher, button maker, and veterinarian . . . now I have to be sex therapist for a guy who gives people a rash."

"It could be fun. Male bonding and all that. And while we're on the subject of sex instruction, I delivered the bag to Jeanine and watched the movie with her."

This got a grin out of Diesel. "Did you like it?"

"It was horrible, but we watched it twice."

Diesel laughed out loud.

"It's the ultimate chick flick. When Dickbender screamed at the end Jeanine turned white and had a third glass of wine. How's the Bernie hunt going?"

"It's not. I can't find him," Diesel said. "I'm getting no vibes at all. Does his wife know how to get in touch with him?"

"No. I left her my card, and she said she'd call if he made contact. How about Annie? Anything on her?"

"Can't find her either," Diesel said. "It's like the two of them have gone to the moon."

"They can't actually do that, can they?"

"Honey, we're a little freaky . . . we're not NASA."

I was hit by a gust of wind, and I hunkered down into my jacket, my breath making frost clouds in front of me. Diesel pulled me close and snuggled me into him, and I instantly felt warm. The heat burned in my chest, curled through my stomach, and headed south.

My voice rose an octave. "What are you doing?"

"I'm warming you," Diesel said.

"I don't need to be *that* warm."

"Hey, I'm just sharing body heat. I can't help it if it gets you all bothered."

"I'm not all bothered."

Diesel smiled down at me.

"Oh crap!" I said, looking up at him. "You've got dimples."

"That isn't all I've got."

I jumped away. "I'm leaving. I'm going to check on Charlene Klinger."

9

Charlene was in her little front yard, walking Blackie around in circles, trying to get him to tinkle.

"Maybe he needs a fire hydrant or a tree," I said.

"That's the problem," Charlene said. "He can't put any weight on his front leg, so he falls over if he lifts his back leg."

"How did dinner go last night?"

"Hard to tell. Junior spilled his milk as soon as we sat down to the table, and it made a flood, and we all got dripped on. And when we were trying to mop up the milk, Blackie got the pot roast and ran away with it. So we had peanut butter and jelly for dinner. And while we were eating our sandwiches, Fluffy got loose and ate Gary's shoelaces and left jelly beans under the table.

"I had gotten a movie for when the kids went to bed, but Gary was sort of soaked with milk, so he left early. He looked like he was thinking about kissing me good night at the door, but the kids were all standing there watching, so he shook my hand and left."

"Wow."

"Yeah, it was a night to remember. Maybe we should go to plan B and find me a housewife."

"But he must like you if he was thinking about kissing you when he left."

"I guess."

"Do you like him?"

"Sure. What's not to like? He's nice to the kids and the animals. And he's even nice to me. And he's cute and cuddly. And he seems very stable. I just can't imagine anyone wanting to take on the chaos."

I was used to having dinner with a kid who thought she was a horse, a grandmother who set the tablecloth on fire on a regular basis, and a future brother-in-law who fainted and farted at the mention of marriage. I didn't see where Charlene had more than the normal amount of chaos.

Ralph had been standing in the doorway, taking it all in. "Maybe we should set the cat on fire again," he said. "Just a little."

I told Charlene to hold off on the cat, and I got back into my car and searched through Gary Martin's file for his phone number. I called his home phone and got his machine. I tried his cell and got his message service. The message service said he was in emergency surgery, so I headed for his clinic. Twenty minutes later, I pulled into his lot, looked in my rearview mirror, and saw Diesel pull in behind me.

I got out of the Escape and went back to Diesel. "How do you always know where to find me?"

Diesel shrugged. "I can tune in to you."

"You have my car bugged, don't you?"

Again, the smile with the dimples. Most guys look cute with dimples. Diesel got dimples, and the temperature went up ten degrees.

"Don't you dare dimple me," I said to him.

"Can't help it. It just happens. Do you have Annie's file with you? I need to see it."

I got the file from my car and slid onto the passenger seat, next to Diesel. "Not a lot in this. Just the usual bond agreement and personal information."

Diesel scanned the paperwork. "Annie's lawyer secured her bond from Vinnie. Standard procedure. The lawyer is one of us. She went back to her house in Hamilton Township, and two days later Bernie started harassing her. I was called in, and we moved her out to the safe house. I find it hard to believe someone discovered the safe house. I think Annie must have left voluntarily."

"Have you been back to her house? Maybe she just wanted to go home."

"I sent Flash. He said the house was locked and dark, but I think we should see for ourselves."

I shelved Gary Martin, rammed myself back into the Escape, and followed Diesel across town to Annie's house. It was exactly what I would have expected. A tidy cape with two front dormers. White siding and black shutters. Very traditional. White picket fence around the small yard. A red heart on the mailbox. We parked in the driveway and walked to the front door.

"There's bad energy here," Diesel said.

I took a step back. I didn't want to walk in and find Annie dead on her living room floor. "How bad are we talking about? Do I want to wait out here?"

"Not that bad. *Disrupted* would be a better word."

Diesel opened the door, and we walked into the dark, silent foyer. He flipped a light on, we worked our way through the house, and it was clear that the house had been tossed. Couch cushions were scattered, drawers were left open, beds were torn apart, toilet-tank tops were on the floor. No stone unturned. We checked all the closets, the basement, and the crawl spaces. No bodies found.

We left Annie's house exactly as we found it, Diesel locked the door behind us, and we angled ourselves into his 'vette to talk.

"Someone was looking for something," I said to Diesel.

"Yeah, and there might have been a struggle in the foyer. The vase was knocked off the sideboard onto the floor."

"The obvious person is Bernie, but I don't know why he'd have reason to search the house. Do you suppose the police did this, searching for the supposedly stolen property?"

"No," Diesel said. "This doesn't feel like a police search. And I doubt the police would go to this trouble for a charge I can almost guarantee will be dismissed. Annie's wanted for armed robbery and assault with a deadly weapon. A guy named Stanley Cramp claims Annie walked into his pawnshop, robbed him, and shot him in the foot. No weapon was found, but two witnesses can place Annie at the scene. Neither of them saw the robbery or assault happen."

Diesel was turned toward me in the small car. His arm was resting on my seat back, and he was absentmindedly stroking my neck with his fingertip while he was talking. It was soothing and disturbingly erotic, all at the same time, and I was working hard to pay attention to the conversation and not to the warm fingertip.

"Why was Annie in a pawnshop?" I asked Diesel.

"Annie said she went into the pawnshop on a whim. She said she saw a necklace in the window that intrigued her. The two witnesses were in the shop when she went in. The witnesses left. Annie left shortly after that without the necklace. And minutes later the call went in to 911."

"How was she identified?"

"She'd parked in front of the shop, and Stanley Cramp took her plate down."

"What is she accused of taking?" I asked Diesel.

"The necklace. Nothing else."

"Have you talked to Stanley Cramp?"

"Not yet, but I think it's time. I'd like you to do it. See if you can charm something out of him. If that doesn't work, feel free to shoot him in the other foot."

"That would be tough," I told him, "since I haven't got a gun."

Diesel reached under his seat and pulled out a Glock.

"I'm not going to take that!" I said.

"Why not?"

"I hate guns."

"You can't hate guns. You're a bounty hunter."

"Yes, but I almost never shoot people. Bounty hunters only shoot people on television."

Diesel raised an eyebrow.

"Okay, so maybe I shot a couple guys, but it wasn't my fault."

"Just take the friggin' gun," Diesel said. "Stanley Cramp isn't a nice person."

"Where am I going to find this guy?"

"He lives in an apartment over the pawnshop, but at this time of day he'll be working. The pawnshop is a one-man operation, open seven days a week."

I got out of Diesel's 'vette and into my Escape. I drove into the center of the city and took the side street that led to the pawnshop. I parked two doors down on the opposite side of the street. I left my car, crossed the street, and glanced at Diesel parked one store down. I rang the bell next to the front door and got buzzed in. High security.

Stanley Cramp looked like life had pretty much been sucked out of him. He was about five foot nine and scrawny. Mid-fifties with thinning oily black hair that was badly in need of a cut. His clothes were a size too large. His teeth were tobacco-stained. He had bloodhound bags under his eyes and skin the color and texture of wet cement. He looked like he'd be better placed in a body bag than standing behind the counter in a pawnshop.

I approached the counter and sent Cramp a flirty smile, and Cramp turned to see if someone was standing behind him.

"I hope you don't mind," I said to him. "I was freezing out there, and your shop looked cozy and warm. And I saw you in here all by yourself."

"You aren't looking to . . . you know, make money, are you? Because I think you're real cute, but I don't have any money. I bet on the wrong horse yesterday, and I got cleaned out."

Oh great, he thought I was a hooker. Not exactly a flattering appraisal, but I could get some mileage out of it. "Do you bet on the wrong horse a lot?"

"Yeah, unfortunately. I used to always win, and then my luck turned, and now I keep getting deeper and deeper in the crapper."

"Jeez, that's too bad. Still, you're lucky you have this pawnshop. Is it yours?"

"Yeah, sort of. I owe some people money, but I'll take care of that as soon as my luck changes."

I wandered around, looking in the cases. "You used to have a real pretty necklace in the window, but I haven't seen it lately."

"The one with the red stone? It got stolen. Some lady came in and robbed me and shot me in the foot."

"Get out!"

"Honest to God. I still can't get a shoe on that foot."

"That's horrible. Did she get arrested?"

"Yeah, but the cops didn't recover the necklace."

"Wow."

"I got a bottle of real good hooch behind the counter," Cramp said. "You want some to help get you warmed up?"

"Sure."

Cramp pulled out a bottle of Jack Daniel's and set it on the display case. "Help yourself."

"Do you have a glass?"

"I have glasses upstairs. That's where I live."

"Maybe we could go upstairs."

"Yeah, that'd be real good, but like I told you, I don't have any money."

"Well, what the heck, it's cold, and I don't have anything better to do. Let's go upstairs anyway."

Cramp looked like he was going to keel over.

"But what about the shop?" I asked.

"I'll close it," Cramp said, hurrying to the front door, throwing the bolt, changing the sign around to say CLOSED. "There's never much business on Sunday anyway." He took the bottle of Jack and motioned me to the rear of the pawnshop. "I have stairs that go up to my apartment," he said. "We don't even have to go out."

The stairs were narrow and dark and creaky, leading to a

small apartment that was also narrow and dark and creaky. The front room had a television on a card table, and opposite the television was a daybed covered with a floral quilt. A scarred end table had been placed to one side of the daybed.

Cramp got a couple glasses from the kitchen. He set the glasses on the end table and filled them with the Jack. "Down the hatch," he said, and he emptied his glass.

I sipped demurely at mine. "It's nice up here," I said.

Cramp looked around. "Used to be nicer before my luck changed. I had some real good pieces, but you know how it is when you're in retail. You have to turn a profit when you get a buyer."

"I bet you were sorry to get robbed of the necklace. It looked expensive."

"I wish I never saw that necklace. Look what it got me . . . a shot-up foot."

"I think it's an interesting story. It could probably even be a movie."

"You think?" Cramp poured himself more Jack. "Yeah, I guess it could make a movie."

Okay, I had him. He wasn't a smart guy, and he was a little drunk, and it was going to be easy to get him rolling on an ego trip.

"Who hocked the necklace?" I asked Cramp. "Was it someone glamorous?"

"Well, not movie-star glamorous, but she was okay. In her twenties. Big bazoos. Sort of rat's-nest hair, but when you got bazoos like that it don't matter, right? That's why I remember her. I'm not good with names, but I remember a good rack."

Charming.

"Anyway, it was the same story I hear every day," Cramp said. "She got the necklace from her boyfriend. Her boyfriend turned out to be a jerk. She wants some money for the necklace."

Cramp tossed his Jack down his throat. Glug, glug, glug. This could explain his embalmed appearance.

"Keep going," I said. "I want to hear the rest of the story."

"Sure," he said. "I never thought much about it, but it's a pretty good story. And it gets even better. I hock the piece for Ms. Big Boobs, and a couple weeks down the road this guy comes in and wants the necklace. He's got the claim ticket. I ask him what happened to the girl with the hooters, and he says I should shut my pie hole and give him the necklace.

"Now here's where it gets good. This is the part that would be good for the movie. Almost all the jewelry in the shop is fake. I got a guy who fences the stuff when it comes in and makes me paste. It's a win-win deal for me, right? I get the money from the fence, and then I either sell the paste to a customer, or the idiot who hocked it in the first place buys it back. Most of the time people can't even tell it's fake. And if they suspect it's fake, they're too embarrassed to do anything about it. Pretty smart, hunh? I thought of it all by myself."

"Wow," I said. "Cool."

"Yeah. So anyway, this guy is standing in front of me with the claim ticket for the necklace, and all of a sudden I recognize him. It's Lou Delvina. He's the jerk boyfriend! I mean, Lou Delvina. Jesus. Do you know who Lou Delvina is?"

"I've heard of him," I said to Cramp.

Everyone in Trenton knew Lou Delvina. For twenty years, he was a shooter for the north Jersey mob, and then he got his own real estate and moved into the Trenton area. He wasn't big-time, but he made the most of what he had. I'd heard stories about Delvina, and none of the stories was good. Delvina was a very scary guy.

"If you know who Delvina is, you know the problem I've got," Cramp said. "I sort of stole a necklace from someone who would kill me if he found out. And chances are sort of good he'd find out, since I'm guessing he knows paste when he sees it."

"Jeez," I said. "You must have been messing your pants."

"Big time. But that was when it happened. My luck swung around. Delvina's standing there with his claim ticket, and he gets a phone call. And it's not a good call because his face gets all red and his eyes get beady and squinty. Little rat eyes. And he tells me he has to go, but he'll be back for the necklace, and I should take real good care of it."

"I would have left town," I said to Cramp.

"See, that's what most people would think, but I'm smarter than that. A couple women came into the shop to browse. Locals. And then another woman came in all by herself. And I knew she wasn't local because I saw her park. Right in front. So as soon as they all left I faked a robbery. Good, right?"

"Definitely movie stuff. I bet Brad Pitt could play your part."

"Brad Pitt would be good," Cramp said. "I could see Brad Pitt doing it."

"What did you do with the necklace? Did you plant it on the woman?"

"No. I trashed the necklace. There's a crawl space under the back room, and I threw it down there. I threw the gun down there after I shot myself, too."

"You shot yourself?"

"Yeah, I got carried away. I wanted to make it look real, but it hurt like a bitch. I didn't think it would hurt so much. Anyway, I guess it was worth it because everyone bought the story. I told everybody the lady walked out with the necklace. The cops went after her, and Delvina went looking for her, too. Delvina really wants that necklace."

"Does the real necklace still exist?"

"Hell, no. The stones got reset right away. I don't know what my guy does with the setting. Melt it down, maybe." Cramp looked at the bottle of Jack. Almost empty. "You think we can get to it now?"

"To it?"

"Yeah, you know, the thing we came up here for."

I felt my cell phone buzz in my bag. I retrieved the phone and answered the call.

"Are you okay?" Diesel asked.

"Yeah."

"Do you need help?"

"There's no emergency, but assistance might be good at this point. Where are you?"

"I'm just outside the pawnshop."

"It's locked."

"Not anymore." And he disconnected.

"Who was that?" Cramp asked.

"My pimp."

"Jesus, I told you and told you I don't have any money. What do you want? Take anything in the shop. How about some jewelry? It's all fake but it's still good shit."

Diesel strolled into the front room and looked at Cramp, and I could see Cramp start to sweat through his shirt.

"Is there a problem?" Diesel asked.

"No problem," Cramp said. "I told her to take anything she wanted from the shop. Hell, she didn't even do anything."

Diesel slid a look my way. "Is that right?"

I shrugged.

Cramp looked at Diesel. "Are you going to hit me?"

"Maybe," Diesel said.

Cramp's nose was running and his eyes were red-rimmed and tearing up. I was starting to feel sorry for him. He was such a pathetic little worm.

"You aren't a cop, are you?" Cramp asked me.

"No. I'm not a cop."

Cramp looked over at Diesel.

"He's not a cop either," I said. "Actually, I'm not sure *what* he is."

Diesel didn't crack a smile. "Do we have any more business here?"

"No. He hasn't got any money."

"Then it looks to me like we're done here," Diesel said. "Let's roll."

"Here's a parting message," I said to Cramp. "If it looks too good to be true, it probably is."

Diesel wrapped his arm around my neck when we got outside. "What was with the profound message?"

"He thought I was a hooker and he was going to get a freebie."

Diesel hugged me to him. "The guy's a moron. Anyone can see you're not the sort of girl who gives freebies."

"Gee, thanks. I told him you were my pimp."

"Lucky me."

"He has the supposedly stolen necklace and the assault gun in a crawl space under the back room. Do you think we should get it?"

"No, but I think you should call it in to Morelli. Let him send someone over to retrieve it."

I filled Diesel in on Delvina.

"Good work," Diesel said. "You learned a lot."

"And what about Annie? Do you think it's possible that Delvina has Annie?"

"I think it's possible that Delvina tossed Annie's house and wants the necklace. I don't see how Delvina could get to Annie."

"Coincidence? Maybe she stepped out for air, and he happened to be driving down the street."

"That's a *big* coincidence."

"I haven't got anything else."

"Me either," Diesel said. "Let's talk to Mr. Delvina."

"Oh no. *You* can talk to Delvina. You're Iron Man. And you don't live here. I'm just wimpy Stephanie from the Burg. If Delvina shoots holes in me, all my vital fluids will leak out, and I'll end up looking like Stanley Cramp."

"Wouldn't want any fluids to leak out of you that weren't supposed to," Diesel said. "I'll track Delvina, and you check on Annie's couples. We're coming up on Valentine's Day. Don't want any snafus."

10

My phone rang while I sat in my car watching Diesel drive away.

"Hey, cupcake," Morelli said. "Just checking in. Anything I need to know?"

"Speak of the devil. I was just going to call you. I have some information to share. Vinnie bonded out a woman named Annie Hart. She supposedly robbed a pawnshop and shot the owner in the foot."

"I remember that," Morelli said. "The pawnshop owner is a little weasel named Stanley Cramp."

"Yeah. Turns out Cramp faked the robbery and shot himself in the foot. The gun and the necklace are in a crawl space under the back room. I can give you more details later, but you should get someone over there before Cramp decides to get rid of the evidence."

"I'll call it in. How's everything else?"

"It's really slow at the bonds office. Only one big outstanding . . . and that was Annie Hart. Bob is good. He's visiting with my parents today. Diesel's in town."

"Diesel?"

"Yeah, you remember Diesel, right?"

"Ranger's half-brother."

"He's not Ranger's half-brother."

"He might as well be. They both run in the fast lane with their lights off."

"You used to do that."

"No. I was an asshole. I never actually thought I was Batman."

"I see your point."

"I'm locked away in a sleazoid motel, doing my cop thing. Do I need to come home?"

"Nope. I've got it all under control."

"Good to know," Morelli said. "I should have this wrapped up Tuesday or Wednesday. See you then." And he disconnected.

I cut down to Klockner Boulevard and then to Hamilton and left-turned into the Burg. I eased to a stop in front of my parents' house and killed the engine. Grandma was at the storm door, looking out at me, driven there by some mysterious inner radar that tells her when a granddaughter is approaching. Not that different from Diesel, when you think about it.

"Just in time," Grandma said to me, holding the door open. "Your sister is here, and we got a nice coffee cake from the bakery."

Bob heard my voice and came thundering down the hall, ears flopping, tongue out, google-eyed. He slid on the polished wood floor and plowed into me, knocking me into the wall.

I scratched his head and gave him a hug, and he galloped back to the kitchen and the coffee cake.

"He's been such a good boy," Grandma said. "It makes a house feel like a home when you got a dog in it. And he didn't hardly eat anything this time. The *TV Guide* and a loaf of bread, but the good thing was he horked up the plastic wrap."

Valerie was at the little kitchen table. She had the baby on her lap and coffee in front of her.

"Where are the girls?" I asked.

"Playgroup," Valerie said. "They go every day now."

I sliced off a chunk of coffee cake and out of habit I stood at the sink to eat.

My mother put a plate and fork and napkin on the table. "Sit," she said. "It's not good for your digestion to eat at the sink. You eat too fast. You don't even chew. Did you chew that piece of cake?"

I didn't know if I'd chewed it. I couldn't even remember eating it, but my hand was empty, and I had crumbs on my shirt, so I guess that said it all.

I pulled a chair out across from Valerie and sat down. It was too late to eat my cake in a civilized manner . . . unless I had a second piece. I checked out the waistband on my jeans. Snug. Shit.

"Sorry I made Albert faint at the table," I said to Valerie. "I thought he was sort of over the marriage phobia."

"It's hideous," Valerie said. "The man is never going to marry me. I didn't mind at first. I thought he just needed time. Now I don't know what he needs."

"He needs his head examined," Grandma said.

"He had it examined," Valerie said. "They didn't find anything."

We all pondered that for a moment.

"Anyway, it's important that we get married," Valerie said. "I'm pregnant again."

We were all dumbfounded.

"Is that good news?" Grandma asked.

"Yes. I want to have another baby with Albert," Valerie said. "I just wish I was married."

Okay, that was the deal-breaker. Albert Kloughn was going down. He was going to marry my sister. I was going to make it happen.

I scraped my chair back. "Gotta go. Things to do. People to see. Is it okay if I leave Bob here just a little longer?"

"He's not here forever, is he?" my mother asked.

"No! I'll be back for him. I promise."

I hurried out of the kitchen and drove the short distance to Jeanine's house. Her date was due to arrive any minute, and I thought it wouldn't hurt to do a last-minute courage check. I parked in front of her house, ran to the door, and rang the bell.

The door was thrown open, and Jeanine stood there buck naked. "Ta daaaah!" she sang out.

We locked eyes, and we both let out a shriek. I clapped

my hands over my eyes, and Jeanine slammed the door shut. A minute later, the door reopened and Jeanine appeared, wrapped in a blanket.

"I thought you were Edward," she said.

"How much have you had to drink?"

"Enough. And you'll be happy to learn I watched the movie three more times and practiced moaning." Her eyes rolled back in her head. "Ohhhh," she moaned. "Oh yeah. Oh yeah." She opened her eyes and looked at me. "How was that?"

A door opened two doors down, and an elderly man looked out at us. He shook his head and muttered something about lesbians and retreated back into his house.

"That was pretty good," I said, "but you might want to adjust the volume."

"Do you think the naked greeting is too much? I figured I'd get it over and done, so we could make our six o'clock dinner reservation. I was afraid if I waited until after dinner I'd get nervous and throw up."

"Glad to see you've got it all figured out."

Jeanine took a deep breath and cracked her knuckles. "Maybe I need another drinky poo."

"Probably you've had enough drinky poos," I told her. "You don't want to get horizontal until your date shows up."

I jogged back to the Escape, slipped behind the wheel, and punched in Charlene Klinger's number.

"He called," she yelled into the phone. "He wants to take me to dinner. What do I do?"

"You go to dinner with him."

"It's not that simple. I don't know what to wear. And I need a babysitter. Where am I going to get a babysitter at this late notice?"

"I'm on my way," I told her, putting the car in gear. "I'll be there in a half hour."

Junior opened the front door and let me in.

"Where's your mom?" I asked.

"Upstairs. She's going nuts because she can't find anything to wear, and she got her hair stuck in a torture device."

I trooped upstairs and found Charlene in the bathroom with a curling iron in her hand.

"Stephanie Plum, full-service matchmaker, available for wardrobe consultation and babysitting," I told Charlene.

"Are you sure you can handle the kids?" she asked me.

"Piece of cake."

Truth is, I'd rather get run over by a truck than spend an hour with Charlene's kids, but I didn't know what else to do.

"I thought I'd wear this pants suit," she said. "What do you think?"

"The pants suit is good, but the shirt isn't sexy."

"Oh God, am I supposed to be sexy?"

I ran to her bedroom and sifted through the pile of clothes on her bed. I found a V-necked sweater that I thought had potential and brought it into the bathroom.

"Try this," I told her.

"I can't wear that. It's too low. I bought it by mistake."

I unbuttoned her out of the shirt and dropped the sweater over her head. I took a step back, and we both looked in the mirror.

Charlene had *a lot* of cleavage. "Perfect," I said. "Now you're a domestic goddess *and* a sex goddess."

Charlene looked down at her boobs. "I don't want to give him the wrong idea."

"And that would be, what?"

"I don't know. I'm not good at this. I never have a second date. Everyone always disappears halfway through the *first* date. What am I supposed to do on a second date? Should I . . . you know?"

"No! You don't *you know* until the third date. And then, only if you really like the guy. I've had years where I didn't *you know* at all."

Junior was watching. "Boy, you have a lot of skin," he said to his mother. "And your hair looks funny."

Charlene's attention moved from her boobs to her hair. "I got the curling iron caught in it, and some of it got singed off."

I finger-combed some conditioner into Charlene's singed hair and fluffed her out with a round brush and hair dryer.

"You must not be a Jersey native," I said to Charlene.

"I moved here five years ago from New Hampshire."

That would explain the hair.

I pulled some lip gloss and blush out of my bag and

swiped some on Charlene. The doorbell rang, and Charlene gripped the bathroom counter for support.

"Remember," I said to her, "you're a goddess."

"Goddess," she repeated.

"And you don't put out until the third date."

"Third date."

"Unless he gets carried away with your cleavage and asks you to marry him . . . then you could accelerate the process."

I walked Charlene down the stairs and helped her get into a coat. I told Gary Martin to behave himself and get Charlene home before her ten o'clock curfew. And I closed the door after them and turned to face her kids.

"I'm hungry," Ralph said.

The other three stared at me in sullen silence.

"What?" I said to them.

"We don't need a babysitter," Russell said.

"Fine. Pretend I'm something else. Pretend I'm a friend."

Russell looked me up and down.

"How old are you?" I asked him.

"Sixteen."

"I don't think so."

"He's twelve," Ralph said. "And he got a bone in school last week and got sent home."

"It's *boner*, dipshit," Ernie said.

Ralph stood on tiptoes and got into Ernie's face. "Don't call me dipshit."

"Dipshit, dipshit, dipshit."

I looked at my watch. I'd been on duty for three minutes and I'd lost control. This was going to be a long night.

"Everyone into the kitchen," I said. "I'm going to make dinner."

"What are you going to make?" Ralph wanted to know.

"Peanut butter sandwiches."

"I don't like peanut butter," Ralph said.

"Yeah, and that's not dinner. That's lunch," Ernie said. "We need to have meat and vegetables for dinner."

I took my phone out and dialed Pino's Pizza. "I need three large pies with peppers, olives, onions, and pepperoni," I told them. "And I need it fast." I gave them the address and turned back to the kids. "Vegetables and meat, coming up."

"I'm going upstairs," Russell said.

Ernie followed. "Me, too."

Junior ran off to the back of the house and disappeared.

"You have to feed Kitty and Blackie and Fluffy and Tom and Fritz and Melvin. And you can't give Blackie any pizza because he's lactose internet."

"Do you mean lactose intolerant?"

"Yeah. He gets the squirts. He squirts all over everything."

I went to the kitchen, and I put some cat crunchies in a bowl for Kitty and some dog crunchies in a bowl for Blackie and some rabbit pellets in a bowl for Fluffy.

"Tom and Fritz and Melvin are the outside cats," Ralph said. "Mom can't catch them, so she just feeds 'em."

I fed the outside cats and realized I hadn't seen Junior in a while.

"Where's Junior?" I asked Ralph.

Ralph shrugged. "Junior runs away a lot," he said.

I yelled for Junior, but Junior didn't show. Ralph and I went upstairs to look for Junior and found Russell and Ernie surfing porn sites.

"They do this all day long," Ralph said. "It's why Russell gets bones."

"It's *boner*," Ernie said. "Bone-*errrr*!"

"Doesn't your mom have parental controls on this computer?" I asked Russell.

"They're broken," Russell said.

"Russell's a geek," Ralph said. "He can break anything. He broke the television so we can watch naked people."

"Anyway, my mother doesn't care what I do," Russell said. "It's not like I'm a kid."

"Of course you're a kid," I said to him. "Shut that off."

"I don't have to," Russell said. "You're not my mother. You can't tell me what to do."

I punched Diesel's number into my phone.

"Help," I said when he answered.

"What's up?"

"I'm babysitting for Charlene, and I've lost a kid, and two more are surfing porn sites, and it's going to look real bad if I have to shoot them."

"I'm not actually a kid person," Diesel said.

"I ordered pizza."

"Honey, you need to come up with something better than pizza as a bribe."

"Okay, you can sleep in the bed . . . but you have to stay on your side."

"Deal."

Diesel and the pizza arrived at the same time. Diesel paid the delivery kid and brought the pizza inside. He dropped the three boxes on the table, opened one, and took a piece.

"You have one kid sitting at the table," Diesel said. "Where are the others?"

"Two are upstairs and refuse to come down. I can't find Junior."

Diesel stood silent for a moment. He turned slightly and looked around the room. He ate some of his pizza and popped the top on a can of soda. "He's under the sink," Diesel said.

I opened the under-the-sink cabinet door and peeked in at Junior. "Do you want pizza?"

"Can I eat it in here?"

I gave him a piece of pizza on a paper towel and closed the door on him.

"Can I have a piece?" Ralph asked.

"Knock yourself out," Diesel said. "I'm going to get your brothers."

Ralph and I helped ourselves to pizza, and Diesel disappeared up the stairs. There was a lot of kid yelling followed by silence. Moments later, Diesel ambled into the kitchen with Russell and Ernie. He had both of them by the backs of their shirts, and their feet weren't touching the floor.

Diesel plunked Russell and Ernie down and selected a second piece of pizza. "Looks like I'm going to be here for a while," he said to Russell and Ernie. "Might as well make it worthwhile. Do you guys play poker? Have you got any money?"

Diesel, Russell, Ernie, and Ralph were still at the kitchen table when Charlene got home. I was watching television. Junior was asleep on the couch next to me.

"How'd it go?" I asked Charlene.

"I think this was the first time in five years no one spilled milk at dinner. It felt weird. And he kissed me good night at the door. That felt weird, too, but I liked it. He's a really nice man."

"Is he your true love?"

"Too early to tell, but he has potential. He's invited me and the kids to his house for dinner tomorrow night."

Diesel meandered in from the kitchen. "Just in time," he said to Charlene. "We were playing pepperoni poker, and we ran out of pepperoni."

Ralph was trailing behind Diesel. "He won all the pepperonis, and then he ate them," Ralph said.

I raised an eyebrow at Diesel.

"I'm good at cards," Diesel said.

"You were playing with kids!"

"Yeah, but they cheat."

"He said if he caught us cheating again, he'd turn us into toads," Ralph said. "He can't do that, can he?"

"What's with this toad thing?" I said to Diesel.

"Idle threat," Diesel said. "Sort of."

I stuffed myself into my jacket and hung my bag on my shoulder. "Have fun tomorrow night," I told Charlene. "Keep in touch."

Diesel followed me out and walked me to my car.

"What's happening with Annie?" I asked him.

"Can't find her. Can't find Bernie. And now I can't find Lou Delvina. He has a house in Cranberry, but the only one in the house is his wife. There's a two-car garage with just one car in it. I have someone checking on other properties. He's not at his social club. He's not at his place of business."

"It's only nine o'clock. He could be lots of places."

"True. I have Flash watching his house."

My phone buzzed.

"Thank the Lord I got you," Lula said. "You're not gonna believe this one, and don't hang up because this is my one phone call."

11

"Where are you?" I asked Lula.

"I'm in jail. Where the heck do you think I am with one phone call? Anyways, I need someone to bond me out of here."

"I'll have to get Connie. Vinnie left for his Valentine's cruise with Lucille." I looked at my watch. "It's nine o'clock Sunday night. Connie's going to have to get a judge out of his jammies to set bond. What are the charges?"

"Destruction of personal property and tying a idiot's dick in a knot. And Tank's here, too."

Tank was second in command at Ranger's security company. He was Ranger's best friend, and he watched Ranger's back. He was a big guy who didn't talk much but carried a real big stick. From time to time Lula managed to snag him and have her way, and the next morning Tank would look like the living dead. To my knowledge this was the first time she'd gotten him arrested.

"Tank and me were at this bar," Lula said. "And some drunk-ass moron started on Tank. How Tank had no neck.

And how Tank looked like Shrek, except Tank wasn't green. And I was getting real annoyed because okay, all that's true, but I didn't like this guy's attitude, you see what I'm saying? And then he started calling me Shrek's fat 'ho . . . and that's when I hit him. And things sort of went in the toilet after that."

Diesel was smiling when I disconnected. "Ranger's gonna be pissed. He works hard to keep a clean, low profile."

"You know Ranger?"

"From a distance."

I called Connie and told her about Lula and Tank.

"Can you get them out?" I asked Connie.

"Probably. I'll have to make some phone calls. I'll get back to you."

Diesel and I got into my Escape. I turned the heat on high, and Diesel cracked his window.

"How do you know Ranger?" I asked him.

Diesel shrugged. "I hear things. I assume Connie is buying a judge?"

"This is a small community. We try to be civilized to each other. Connie will call in a favor."

Diesel was looking relaxed next to me, but I knew his priority was to find Annie, and it had to be on his mind.

"I know you're worried about Annie," I said. "Am I keeping you from whatever it is that you do?"

"I have wheels turning. I'll need to move when I get a call. Until then, I'm all yours."

Connie called back. "I've got the paperwork in motion. I'm going to pick it up now, and I'll meet you at the booking desk in a half hour. I'm assuming Lula and Tank are being held at the station."

"Yep. Ten-four." I turned to Diesel. "This is going to take some time. Would you mind picking Bob up at my parents' house and bringing him home for me?"

"No problem. Call me if you run into trouble."

The Trenton police are housed in a redbrick bunker in a part of town that knows a lot about crime firsthand, mandating that police cars be locked in a lot surrounded by razor wire. Unfortunately, Connie and I didn't qualify for the razor-wire lot and were forced to park on the street, which was more or less a supermarket for chop-shop scouts. Connie drove over in a crapola Beetle she kept for just such an occasion. I got two fake antennae and a big fake diamond-encrusted cross out of my console. I hung the cross on my mirror, and I stuck the antennae to the roof rack. If you didn't look too close you'd think I was a dealer and would most likely kill you if I caught you messing with my car.

It was after normal business hours, so we had to get ourselves buzzed in. Connie was already processing the release when I arrived. There wasn't a lot going on. Too late for rush-hour road rage and too early for drunken domestic violence. A lone sad-sack gangbanger sat chained to a chair that was bolted to the floor. The amount of snot on his shirt suggested he'd been pepper-sprayed.

My buddy Eddie Gazarra was on duty behind the desk. "Sorry about Lula and Tank," he said. "I wasn't here when they came in, or I would have called you right away. Some numbskull rookie dragged their asses in here, and there wasn't anything we could do once they were booked."

"It's okay," I said. "We'll get them bonded out."

Gazarra went back to the holding cell and got Lula and Tank.

"There's no justice to this world," Lula said. "I get taken to jail, and the meany that called me a fat 'ho isn't even here."

"He's at the hospital getting his nuts extracted from his nose," Gazarra said. "He'll get charged as soon as he can walk without spitting up blood."

"How about me?" Lula said. "I got a scratch on my arm, and I'm gonna get a bruise, too. And this here's a new sweater that someone grabbed hold of and tore a hole in."

Tank wasn't saying anything. He took his belt and shoelaces and pocketed the plastic bag with his incidentals . . . wallet, keys, loose change.

"More bad news," Gazarra said. "They towed and impounded a red Firebird that was parked illegally in a handicap space in front of the bar."

"That's my baby!" Lula said. "And it wasn't parked illegal. It had two inches sticking over the line. There was only two inches in the dumbass handicap spot."

Gazarra passed me a piece of paper. "Here's the address for the impound lot and the citation for the car. My advice is to pick it up tomorrow, because your girlfriend here is probably blowing over the alcohol limit, and with the kind of luck she's having, she'll be brought back here for DUI."

We all trudged out of the station, happy to find both cars still at the curb, unmolested. Connie zipped away, hoping to catch her television show, and I loaded Tank and Lula into my Escape.

"How about you?" I said to Tank. "Did you drive to the bar?"

Tank just looked at me.

I couldn't hold the smile back. "You drove there in a Rangeman vehicle, didn't you?"

Tank nodded. "Ranger's gonna kill me."

"Ranger doesn't have to know."

"Ranger knows everything," Tank said. His eyes held mine. *"Everything."*

Oh boy.

"What bar did you two trash?"

"Sly Dog," Tank said. "The car's in the lot alongside the bar."

Sly Dog was a watering hole for people coming to and going from events at the Sovereign Bank Arena. The complexion of the bar changed according to the event, and I wasn't sure what was going on tonight. Could have been a rock concert or a hockey game or monster trucks. It sat just outside the Burg, and was maybe a half mile from Lula's apartment.

I took Perry Street to Broad Street and sailed through the center of the city, coming up behind the arena and the bar. I pulled into the lot and parked behind the black Rangeman SUV.

Lula was in the seat beside me, and Tank was in the back. I slid a look at Lula. "Is there a plan?"

"Hey, Shrek," Lula yelled back to Tank. "You got a plan?"

"Guess I should take you home," Tank said.

"Yeah," Lula said. "That would be the polite thing to do. Might have to stop at the drugstore on the way. Wouldn't want to run out of . . . you know, *anything*."

I checked Tank out in the rearview mirror, and our eyes met, and he smiled.

It was eleven o'clock by the time I got home. Lights were off in my apartment with the exception of a nightlight burning in the bathroom, throwing light into the bedroom. Diesel and Bob were asleep in bed, side by side. Diesel was bare skin for as far as I could see with an arm thrown over Bob.

I slipped into the bathroom and changed into a T-shirt and boxers. I tiptoed to the other side of the bed and crept in next to Bob.

"Did everything work out okay?" Diesel asked, his voice soft in the dark room.

"Yeah. We bonded them out, and then they went home together. This is probably a strange thing to say, but it was . . . nice. I think they really like each other."

"They're lucky."

"Is there someone like that for you? Someone you really like?"

"Right now I really like you. And I'd like you even better if you'd swap places with Bob."

"No way."

"Had to try," Diesel said.

At one o'clock, Diesel's cell phone rang. By the time I was awake and oriented, Diesel was in the middle of a conversation with the caller.

"Don't lose him," Diesel said. "Double-team if you have to and call me if he moves."

I was half sitting, propped on one elbow. "What was that?" I asked when Diesel put his phone back on the night table.

"Lou Delvina just rolled in. Parked in the driveway and scratched himself all the way from the car to his house. Flash said he got a good look at him through the kitchen window, and Delvina is covered with hives."

"Bernie!"

"Yeah, looks like it. Don't know how they're connected, but it can't be friendly if Delvina is scratching."

Bob had moved off the bed sometime during the night, and there was a big empty space between Diesel and me.

Diesel patted the space. "You could move over here," he said.

"I don't think so."

"It's warm and comfy."

"I'm warm enough."

"I could make you warmer."

"Jeez," I said. "You never give up."

"It's one of my better qualities."

It was bright sunshine when I opened an eye to Diesel. He was standing at bedside, showered and shaved and wearing a clean shirt.

"Where'd the clean shirt come from?" I asked.

"Flash brought me some clothes this morning."

"Where'd Flash get the clothes?"

"I don't know. Didn't ask."

"And you shaved. What's the occasion?"

"It's Valentine's Day. I wanted to be ready in case you got all romantic on me."

Valentine's Day. How could I forget! I dragged myself out of bed and looked at the clock. Nine. I did a sigh.

"Have a tough night?" Diesel asked.

"I don't want to talk about it."

"I could have made it a good night."

I narrowed my eyes at him. "I said I *don't* want to talk

about it. I'm feeling cranky. Give me some room. And stop smiling at me with those damn dimples."

He handed me a mug of hot coffee. "I'm just trying to get your blood circulating. We have a man in motion. Lou Delvina left his house ten minutes ago. Flash is a beat behind him. I'm heading out. Do you want to be in on this?"

"No. Yes."

Diesel was hands on hips, looking down at me.

"Yes," I said. "Give me a minute."

"Forty seconds would be better."

I picked some clothes off the floor and ran into the bathroom with them. I was dressed and out in record time with a hairbrush in my hand. I grabbed a ball cap off the dresser and rammed my feet into boots. Diesel stuffed me into my jacket and handed me a new mug of coffee, and we were out of the apartment, down the hall to the elevator.

"Bob!" I said. "What about Bob?"

"I walked him and fed him. He'll be fine. He's sleeping in a patch of sun in the dining room."

We took the 'vette with Diesel driving. He peeled out of the lot and headed west on Hamilton Avenue to Route 1. He took the Route 1 bridge into Pennsylvania, and I looked across to the Warren Street bridge. TRENTON MAKES— THE WORLD TAKES was the message on the bridge. I hadn't a clue what it meant.

"How do you know where you're going?" I asked him.

"I can feel Flash in front of me. There are a couple

people I connect to, and Flash is one of them. I can't always connect, but it's strong today. Probably because he's excited to be on the chase."

"Can you connect to me?"

"Sometimes."

"So you didn't bug my car?"

"No, I didn't bug your car. I dropped the bug into your purse. GPS is more reliable than this hocus-pocus crap. Unless it's raining. I have real problems in the rain. Nothing works in the rain."

We were off Route 1 and heading north toward Yardley. Traffic was moderate. Diesel drove into Yardley and pulled to the side of the road.

"What's up?" I asked him.

"Lost Flash. It feels like he's behind me."

Diesel punched a number into his cell phone. "Lost you," he said. He turned in his seat and looked out the back window. "Yeah," he said, "I see the sign. Get me a couple of those glazed sticks and coffee." Diesel looked over at me. "Everyone stopped to get doughnuts. Do you want anything?"

"Double your order."

"Make that four glazed sticks and two coffees," Diesel told Flash.

Five minutes later, Diesel pulled back into traffic. "We have a visual," he said. "That's Flash in the blue Honda Civic in front of us. Two cars ahead of him is a black Lincoln with Jersey plates. I imagine that's our man, Delvina."

We followed Flash and Delvina for an additional ten minutes, taking a road that hugged the Delaware River. There were houses on either side of the road. Large older houses on partially wooded lots mixed with small summer cottages. We saw the black Lincoln turn into a riverside driveway and disappear behind a six-foot-high privacy hedge. Flash slowed and parked on the shoulder one house down. We parked behind him and got out of the 'vette. Flash met us halfway with the coffee and doughnuts.

"I don't think you've met," Diesel said. "Flash, Stephanie. Stephanie, Flash."

Flash was maybe five foot ten with spiked red hair and a bunch of diamond studs in his ears. He was slim, and you might place him in high school until you looked closely and saw the fine lines around his eyes. He was wearing jeans and sneakers and a ski jacket with a bunch of lift tickets hooked onto the zipper tag. I suspected he was a boarder.

I took a doughnut and coffee and thought this would be really nice if it was a social occasion. We stood there for a while, drinking coffee and eating doughnuts, waiting to see if the Lincoln was just dropping off or picking up. Fifteen minutes went by.

Diesel finished his coffee and put his cup into the empty doughnut bag. "Time to go to work," he said.

Flash crumpled his cup and added it to the bag. I tossed my remaining coffee and trashed my cup.

"There were two guys in the Lincoln," Flash said. "Delvina and a driver. Delvina came home under his own power last night and parked in the garage. This morning, the Lincoln picked him up. The driver looks like old muscle."

"It would be better if we could do this in the dark," Diesel said, "but I don't want to wait that long."

We were standing in front of Delvina's next-door neighbor's house. It was a large colonial with a shake roof and cedar siding, no gated drive, and no privacy hedge. No lights on inside the house. There was still a dusting of snow left on the driveway. No tire tracks in the snow. The walk hadn't been salted or shoveled. Clearly, no one was living there at this time of the year. There was a patch of woods, maybe thirty feet wide, between the two houses.

"No one's in this cedar house," I said. "We can sneak along the tree line and scope things out."

Diesel beeped the 'vette locked, and we walked the cedar house property until Delvina's house could be seen peeking through the vegetation. We moved into the patch of woods to get a better look, trying to stay hidden behind scrubby evergreens.

The Delvina house was large and rambling. Two stories. The house had a four-car garage, but the Lincoln was parked in a circular drive, by the front door. There weren't a lot of windows on this side of the house. A small window up and a small window down. Most likely bathrooms. Interior plantation shutters, closed tight. Another upstairs window with drapes. Bedroom, no doubt. A large swath of frozen lawn lay between us and the house.

"We need to see inside the house," Diesel said. "We need a head count."

"Hang tight," Flash said. "This is a job for the Flashman."

Flash ran across the lawn, plastered himself against the building, and stood listening.

"Is speed his Unmentionable thing?" I asked Diesel.

"So far as I know he's not Unmentionable. He just runs fast."

Flash was creeping around the house, periodically stopping and listening, looking in windows. He turned a corner and disappeared, and Diesel and I waited patiently. Five minutes passed and my patience started to evaporate.

"Chill," Diesel said to me. "He's okay."

A couple minutes later, Flash popped into view and sprinted across the lawn, back to us.

"Delvina and his driver are in there. They're both covered with hives. They've got some kind of white cream on, but it's obviously not helping. Annie is there. She looks okay, except she has hives, too. She's wearing an ankle bracelet with a long length of chain that's attached to something in another room. I think it's a powder room. I couldn't really be sure from my angle. Everyone is in the back of the house, in the family room that's part of the kitchen. And there's another guy in chains. I think it must be Bernie. I've never seen Bernie in person, but I've seen his picture, and I think this is Bernie. I can't see the birthmark because he's also covered in hives, and his face is dotted with the white cream."

"'That's weird," Diesel said. "Why would Bernie give himself hives?"

"I don't know," Flash said, "but these aren't happy people. They're all talking at the same time and waving their hands around and scratching."

"Anyone else in the house?" Diesel asked.

"Not that I could see."

"I need to get in the house, and bring Annie and Bernie out," Diesel said. "I don't want to go in like gangbusters and take a chance on someone getting hurt. I need a diversion."

Now I knew why I'd been invited along. "I guess that would be me," I said.

Diesel handed me the keys to the 'vette. "Do a damsel in distress routine. If you can draw them to the front of the house, we can go in the back."

I ran to the 'vette and took the wheel. I waited until there were no cars in sight, pulled around the Civic, and right-turned hard into Delvina's drive. The property wasn't gated, but the hedge had been carved into a topiary column on either side of the driveway entrance. I deliberately put the 'vette into a skid that took out Delvina's topiary column and positioned the car well into the yard. I fought the airbag and lurched out of the slightly bashed-in 'vette.

I pasted what I hoped was a dazed expression on my face and started up the driveway toward the house. I was halfway there when the door opened, and Delvina's driver looked out at me.

"What the hell was that?" he asked.

I did my best lower-lip tremble, and thought about sad things like roadkill and orphaned birthday cakes left at the bakery, and managed to sort of get a tear going down my cheek. Truth is, the tear was a challenge, but the trembling was easy. It was starting from my knees and working its way up all by itself. For the better part of my life I'd heard stories about Lou Delvina, and they all involved a lot of blood.

"I don't know what happened," I said. "All of a sudden the car went into a skid, and I h-h-hit the hedge."

Delvina appeared behind his driver, and my heart jumped into my throat.

"What the fuck happened to my hedge?" Delvina yelled.

"She skidded into it," his driver said.

"Sonovabitch. You know how hard it is to grow a hedge that size?"

"I'm really sorry," I said. "I must have hit some ice on the road."

Delvina was power-walking down his driveway, swinging his arms, head stuck forward. He was a sixty-year-old bandy-legged fireplug with a lot of black hair and black caterpillar eyebrows. Hard to tell the normal color of his complexion as it was all red hives and white salve and looked to be purple under the salve.

"I don't fucking believe this," Delvina said. "Is there

anything else that could friggin' go wrong? This whole week is caca."

Delvina marched past me and went straight to his hedge. "Oh jeez, just *look* at this," he said. "One of the plants is all broken. There's gonna be a big hole here until this grows."

I'd sort of gotten over the weak-knee thing, since I'd had a chance to check both guys out and knew they weren't packing. Maybe an ankle holster, but that didn't worry me so much. I'd seen cops try to get their gun out of an ankle holster and knew it involved a lot of swearing and hopping around on one foot. I figured by the time Delvina could get his gun off his ankle I'd be long gone, running down the road. In fact, I was having a hard time not going narrow-eyed and pissy because I'd gone to all the trouble to manufacture a tear and no one was noticing. I mean, it's not every day I can pull that off.

The driver had joined Delvina. "Maybe you could do a transplant or something," the driver said. "You know, one of them grafts."

"Christ, my wife's gonna go apeshit on this. This is gonna ruin her whole garden club standing if we can't get this fixed." Delvina had his hand under his shirt and down the front of his pants. "Oh man, I got hives inside and out. I swear to God, you should just shoot me."

"It's them people," the driver said, scratching his ass. "They're putting the juju on us. I say we dump them in the Delaware."

Delvina looked back at the house. "You could be right.

I'm getting tired of them anyway. And I'm starting to think the heartsy-fartsy lady doesn't have what we want."

Delvina and the driver started to walk back to the house, and so far, I hadn't gotten any kind of a sign from Diesel, mystical or otherwise, that the coast was clear.

"Hey," I yelled to Delvina. "What about my car?"

"What about it?" Delvina asked. "Don't it drive? It don't look so bad to me."

"You got a cell phone, right?" the driver said. "Call your club. You got a new 'vette. You probably belong to a club. Like AAA or something."

The right side of the 'vette was scraped, and the front right light was smushed in. Pieces of hedge were stuck in the headlight and slightly crumpled hood. I got behind the wheel and raced the motor.

Delvina and his driver were hands on hips, looking at me like I was another hive on their backside. It was cold, and they were standing there in shirtsleeves. They weren't excited about doing the backyard mechanic thing. Fortunately, they were full-on chauvinists who couldn't see me for anything more than a dumb bimbo. If Flash had run into the hedge, neither of them would have left the house without a nine rammed into the small of his back. Still, I was trying their patience, and it was only a matter of time before they figured it out and they went for the ankle holster.

I had one eye on Delvina and one eye looking beyond him to the patch of woods. Finally Diesel emerged and gave me a thumbs-up. I did a small head nod to Diesel and blew out a sigh of relief.

"You're right," I said to Delvina. "I guess the car's okay. Sorry about your hedge." And I carefully backed up, changed gears, and rolled down the driveway and out onto the road. I had my teeth clamped into my lower lip, and I was holding my breath. Sprigs of hedge were flying off the grille, and the right front tire was making a grinding sound, but I kept going until I was around a bend in the road.

12

I pulled to the shoulder and sat and waited, and after a couple minutes, the blue Honda Civic came into view. Diesel got out and jogged over to me.

"Are you okay?" he asked.

"Yes. Do you have Annie and Bernie in the Civic?"

Diesel picked some hedge off the windshield wiper. "Yes. Is this car driveable?"

"The right-side tire is making grinding noises."

Diesel checked out the right-side tire and pulled a large piece of hedge from the wheel well.

"That should help," he said. "Hop over the console. I'm driving."

I scrambled into the passenger seat, and Diesel took the wheel. He eased onto the road, drove a short distance, and made a U-turn. Flash did the same. Diesel waved Flash on, and Flash took the lead. We flew past Delvina's house and retraced our route until we were over the bridge and back in Jersey.

"So far as I can tell, Delvina doesn't know about Annie's

apartment," Diesel said. "I'm going to bring Annie and Bernie there to regroup."

"Did Bernie give himself hives?"

"Apparently he went out of control and infected everyone around him, including himself. I didn't get a chance to find out much more than that."

We motored through town, parked in the underground garage, and took the elevator to Annie's floor. Diesel opened the door, and I turned and looked at Flash and grimaced. His face was breaking out in hives.

"Oh shit," Bernie said to Flash. "I'm really sorry. I'm not doing it on purpose, I swear. The rash is just leaking out of me."

Flash scratched his stomach. "They're coming out all over. What do I do?"

"Get away from Bernie and try a cortisone cream," Diesel said.

Flash ran down the hall and punched the elevator button.

Bernie limped into Annie's apartment. "I've got hives on the bottom on my feet," he said to Diesel. "I've got them everywhere. You have to help me. I don't ever want to see another hive."

I was keeping as far away from Bernie as possible. I was in the hallway leading to the bedroom, looking at everyone else in the living room.

"What about Annie?" Diesel said. "Are you going to leave her alone?"

"I've been chained to Annie for two days. I don't ever want to see her again either."

"I thought we bonded," Annie said.

Bernie scratched his arm. "Yeah, maybe. I guess you're okay. I don't know. I can't think straight. I just want to soak in some cold water or something."

"I talked to Betty," I said to Bernie. "She'd like to stay married, but she has some requests."

"Anything! Cripes, look at this. I've got a hive under my fingernail!"

"I'm going to take you home and get you some salve," Diesel said, "but first I need to know about Delvina. How'd he manage to get you and Annie?"

"I was nuts," Bernie said. "I was trying to get to Annie, but you moved her out of her house, and I couldn't find her. So I got this idea that maybe she left something behind that would give me a clue. You know, like an address written on a pad. It happens all the time on television. Problem was, I broke into her house and ran into two goons who were tearing the place apart. I'm so dumb. I just walked right in on them."

"Delvina was the original owner of the necklace," Annie said. "We overheard him and his driver talking and pieced the story together. The necklace had a bank account number engraved on the back of it. It sounded like Delvina was being investigated for tax fraud, and he didn't want the necklace on his property, so he gave it to his girlfriend. When he found out she hocked it he almost had a seizure."

Annie started to scratch her arm and stopped in mid-scratch and rammed her hands into her pockets. "He came really close to getting the necklace back, but for some reason the pawnshop owner decided to fake the robbery. So of course, Delvina came looking for me."

"It was bad timing that I happened along," Bernie said. "They didn't find the necklace in Annie's house, but since I broke in they figured I had to have some connection to Annie. And then they were fooling around and found her number in my cell phone. So one of Delvina's men called her and said he was me."

"He sort of sounded like you," Annie said. "He said he had something important to say to me. I was hoping you'd calmed down and wanted to talk. I didn't want to miss the opportunity."

"Annie didn't want to go far, so they set a meeting for a coffee house half a block away. When she got there, they snatched her," Bernie said.

"Why didn't you take your purse?" I asked Annie.

"I was just walking down the street for a couple minutes," Annie said. "I had some money and my key in my pocket, and I thought I had my phone, but it must have fallen out of my pocket somewhere. I didn't think I needed anything more than that."

"They brought us to Delvina's summer house on the river," Bernie said. "That was Saturday night. They chained us up, and I went sort of gonzo, and everyone broke out in hives, including me. Then Delvina and his two goons packed up and left. I guess they didn't know what to make of the hives. And then the next morning, Delvina and some other guy showed up and started asking about the necklace, but every time they'd come near us the hives would get worse and pretty soon they couldn't stand it anymore and went away. Good thing we were chained to the bathroom, and the chain was long enough to reach to the refrigerator in the kitchen. They came back this morning and next thing, you rescued us."

"How are my last five cases?" Annie asked. "Are they all going to have a good Valentine's Day? Are they on their way to love everlasting?"

"I don't know about the love everlasting," I said. "But I'm pretty sure they'll all have a good Valentine's Day. Except for Albert Kloughn. Kloughn is last up."

"Oh dear," Annie said, "it's getting late."

"Not to worry. I have a plan." I looked over at Bernie. "You've stopped scratching," I said to him.

"I'm too tired to scratch."

Too bad Bernie was so tired. I wouldn't mind driving him to a couple people I knew and spreading some hives around. For starters, there'd be my ex-husband, Dickie Orr, and my arch-nemesis, Joyce Barnhardt.

"I'm going to take you home to your wife," Diesel said to Bernie. "I'm going to drop you off at the curb, and you're on your own."

"You'll do no such thing," Annie said. "You'll drive us to a drugstore so Bernie can get a Valentine's card and a box of candy. And then we'll all go in and make sure things run smoothly between Bernie and Betty."

Annie had good intentions, but I was starting to think she came from the Planet Ick!

"I heard that," Diesel said to me.

"Did not."

"Did so."

"It was a thought!"

"And?"

"It's almost noon," I said to Annie and Diesel. "You can drop me off at my apartment on your way to Bernie's house in Hamilton Township. I need to check on Bob and get my car. Then I have to see if Lula needs a ride to get her Firebird out of impound. And I want to see how Jeanine and Charlene and Larry Burlew are doing. And last but not least, here's my plan for Kloughn and my sister. I thought I'd tell them I was getting married, and I needed them to be witnesses. I'll tell my parents and my grandmother the same thing. Then everyone will congregate at my parents' house. We'll get a justice of the peace to show up, and at the last minute we'll swap me out for Valerie and Albert Kloughn. I'm afraid if I don't fib to them someone will leak to Kloughn, and he'll be on a plane to Buenos Aires."

"Brilliant," Annie said. "I can facilitate the justice of the peace and the paperwork. I have very good connections for that sort of thing."

Diesel looked down at me. "Who's going to be the bogus groom?"

"It's going to have to be you. You're all I've got today."

"Do I get a conjugal night?"

"Afraid not," I told him.

"We'll see," Diesel said.

"We have a lot to accomplish," Annie said. "We should get moving. We can take my car. We won't all fit in Diesel's Corvette."

I called Valerie as soon as I got back to my apartment. "I'm getting married this afternoon," I said to her. "I want you and Albert to be my witnesses."

"Holy cow," Valerie said. "This is so sudden. Who are you going to marry?"

"Diesel."

Silence.

"Hello?" I said to Valerie.

"Are you sure you want to marry him?"

"Yep. Can you come to the wedding?"

"Sure," Valerie said. "What time?"

"Four o'clock. And I'm going to get married at home."

"Does Mom know?"

"Not yet."

"Oh boy."

"Maybe we shouldn't tell her," I said. "Maybe we should just all show up."

"That sounds like a better way to go," Valerie said. "If you give her four hours, she'll hire caterers and a band

and have the house filled with flowers and two hundred people."

"Yeah, but I can count on you and Albert to be there, right?"

"Absolutely. Are you pregnant?"

"Uh, maybe."

"This will be so amazing. We can have our babies together."

"I didn't say for sure."

"I know, and I won't tell anyone. My mouth is zippered shut."

"Thanks, Val."

Bob was in the kitchen, smiling at me.

"Wipe that goofy expression off your face," I said to Bob. "You're not fooling anyone. You ate my couch. There are big holes in all the cushions, and all the insides are coming out."

There was a piece of fiberfill stuck to Bob's lip. I picked it off and dropped it on the floor with all the other big fluffy blobs of fiberfill.

"I hope this works," I said to Bob. "The alternative is stun gun, and I don't think that would look great in Val's wedding album."

I took Bob out for a walk around the block. When he was empty, we drove to the bonds office.

Lula and Connie were huddled together when I walked in.

"Look at this big-ass box of chocolates I got," Lula said,

working her way around a lump of caramel. "I got it from my sweetie for Valentine's Day. This here's gonna be the best Valentine's Day ever."

Connie and Lula had the huge red heart sitting on Connie's desk. The top was off and the box was half empty.

"You better get some before they're all gone," Connie said to me. "We decided this was lunch."

"Which sweetie sent this?" I asked Lula.

"The *big* sweetie," Lula said. "And anyways, I only got one sweetie now. He's my great huge gigantic hunk of burning love. You don't think Ranger will actually kill him, do you?"

"Ranger and Tank are like brothers."

"Yeah, but remember in *The Godfather* where they offed poor Fredo?"

"Ranger's not going to *off* Tank."

I suspected Ranger would privately think the whole jail thing was pretty funny.

"What's up today?" Lula wanted to know.

"I'm going to check on Jeanine and Charlene and Larry Burlew. Want to ride along?"

"Hell yeah. I could use some air after eating all this candy. I'm feeling seasick. And what's with that nasty red thing in the middle of your forehead? You keep scratching at it. And you got another one in the middle of your cheek."

I ran to the bathroom and looked in the mirror. I had hives! Shit. Double shit.

First stop was the drugstore for salve. Second stop was the DMV. Charlene was behind the counter, looking all smiley-faced. She waved when she saw us, and we cut to the front of the line.

"Excuse us," Lula said to a bunch of grumblers. "We're here doing Cupid patrol. And you need a attitude adjustment or Cupid's gonna pass you by this year."

"I want to thank you again for babysitting," Charlene said.

"No problem. Just wanted to make sure everything was okay."

"Better than okay," Charlene said. "What's on your face?"

"See, now isn't that nice," Lula said on the way out of the building. "Don't that make you feel all warm inside? I told you love was in the air."

Next stop was Larry Burlew's butcher shop.

Burlew was waiting on a customer, so Lula and I stepped to the side. I looked across the street at the coffee shop and saw Jet waving to me. She smiled and gave me a thumbs-up. I thumbs-upped her back.

The customer left, and I stepped forward. "How did the dinner work out?" I asked Burlew.

"It was wonderful. The meat was perfect. And we served it with baby carrots and new potatoes. And then last night we made rack of lamb, and it was sensational."

"Yeah, but did you get any?" Lula wanted to know.

"Sure," Burlew said. "There was plenty to go around. We even had leftovers."

Lula cut her eyes to me. "Gonna have to get Diesel to talk to him in private."

"I made restaurant reservations tonight for Jet and me," Burlew said. "It's Valentine's Day." He looked more closely at me. "Do you have hives? You know, they're usually an allergic reaction to something. Have you had any shellfish lately?"

"Have a wonderful night," I said to him, trying really hard not to scratch the hive on my forehead. "Call me if you need any more help."

"Is he a apple dumpling, or what?" Lula said, sliding into the Escape. "That Jet is a lucky woman. Not every girl gets a man who has a way with meat like that."

I looked in my rearview mirror and dabbed on more salve.

It was a workday, and Jeanine would be at the button factory and inaccessible, so I tried calling her on her cell.

"'Lo," Jeanine said.

"It's Stephanie Plum," I told her. "I'm just checking in to see if everything's okay. Why don't I hear any machine noises in the background?"

"I'm home with the worst hangover in the history of the world."

"How'd it go last night?"

"I think it went okay. Can't remember a lot of it, but he was still here when I woke up this morning, so that's a real good sign, right?"

"Right!"

"Turned out he wasn't a virgin, but he wasn't all that experienced either, so we watched the movie together and tried a bunch of stuff, and then I think we passed out. Anyway, he sent me flowers this morning, and we're going out again tonight."

"Wow, that's great, Jeanine. I'm really happy for you."

"Yeah, I'm happy, too, but I'm going to get off the phone and throw up now."

"I think Bob needs to celebrate all this romance shit with a large fries," Lula said. "He's been a real good dog just sitting back there, but he looks hungry."

"Bob ate a couch this morning."

"Well okay, then I need the large fries. I need some carbs and grease to balance out all the chocolate."

I hit the drive-through window at Cluck-in-a-Bucket and got a monster bucket of fries and a couple sodas and a cheeseburger for Bob. I parked in the Bucket lot and tossed Bob his burger.

Diesel pulled up beside me, got out of his 'vette, and leaned in the window. "Oh man, is that a hive on your forehead? Honey, it's *huge*."

"Do you have any?"

"No," Diesel said. "My immune system is exceptionally strong."

"He's good," Lula said. "He found you without a phone call. He's like a white Ranger."

"I'm carrying a bug," I said to Lula.

"You mean like James Bond shit? Like when he gets stuff from one of the alphabet men. Who is it? M? Q? Z?"

"Is there a special Unmentionable guy who makes bugs for you?" I asked Diesel.

"No. I bought the little devil on the Internet. EBay. Got a real good price. Only used once by some guy who thought his wife was cheating. Wanted to let you know Annie has everything arranged. The justice of the peace will be at your parents' house promptly at four."

Lula paused with her fries. "Say what?"

"It's a long story," I said. "The short version is Diesel and I are pretending to get married, so we can get Kloughn to marry Valerie."

"Does Morelli know about this?"

"It's *pretend*."

"I'm not even gonna ask if Ranger knows. Poor ol' Diesel here be dead if Ranger knew."

I looked at Diesel.

"Maybe," Diesel said, "but not likely. It's hard to kill me. I don't have to get dressed up for this, do I?"

"I better be invited to this," Lula said. "I'd be really pissed off if you got married without inviting me. And if you want to keep your job, you better invite Connie, too."

"It's not a real wedding," I told her.

"Hell, I don't care. Pretend. Real. It's a wedding. Is there gonna be cake?"

"No cake."

"What kind of cheap-ass wedding hasn't got cake?"

"She's right," I said to Diesel. "We should have a cake."

"I can see I need to take charge of this," Lula said. "Here's what we gonna do. Drop me off at the office, and I'll round up Connie, and we'll go get a cake. Then you and Diesel and Bob can go welcome the guests, 'cause it's almost four."

"There aren't any guests," I said. "This is a family wedding."

"Whatever," Lula said. "Let's get going."

"How'd it go with Bernie?" I asked Diesel on the way to my parents' house.

"He's back with Betty. At least for a while. And he's lost his ability to give people hives. When we get Kloughn married off, all the loose ends will be tied, and you can have Annie."

"Probably the charges will be dropped by the time I bring Annie in. If not, I'll make sure she's immediately bonded out again, so she doesn't sit in jail."

"Appreciate it," Diesel said. "She's from the Planet Ick, but she's a good person."

13

"This is a surprise," my mother said when Diesel and Bob and I walked through the door. "Are you staying for dinner?" Her eyes got wide. "What's that on your forehead?"

"It's a hive, and we just came to visit."

"You don't get hives," my mother said. "I've never known you to get hives."

Grandma bustled in from the kitchen. "Look at this, it's the big guy! Isn't this a treat."

"Thanks," Diesel said.

I gave him an elbow. "She's talking about Bob."

A car door slammed behind us, and Mary Alice galloped into the house. She was followed by Angie and Albert and Valerie with the baby. They were all dressed up.

"Goodness," my mother said. "What's going on?"

"Did you tell her?" Valerie asked.

"No. I just got here."

"Well, tell her!" Valerie said. "This is so exciting!"

The doorbell rang. It was Annie and the justice of the peace.

"Oh dear," Annie said when she saw my forehead.

Annie was hives from head to toe, but they were fading, and she was uniformly covered in white salve and makeup.

My father was in the living room, watching television. He turned the sound up and hunkered down in his chair.

I looked at Diesel. He was rocked back on his heels, smiling. "Go ahead, honey," he said to me. "Tell them the happy news."

"I'm getting to it," I said.

"What?" Grandma wanted to know. "What?"

"Diesel and I have decided to get married . . . today."

My mother went white and made the sign of the cross. "Holy Mary, mother of God . . ."

"What about Joseph?" Grandma asked.

I could feel panic rising in my throat. I looked to Diesel for help.

"He's out of town," Diesel said.

I inadvertently made a sort of strangling sound. "Ulk."

"It was all I could think of," Diesel whispered. "I'm not good at this crap."

My mother sucked in some air. "You're pregnant," she said.

"No!"

"Isn't this fab?" Valerie gurgled. "Two new babies!"

Now my father was on his feet. "Babies? Who's having babies?"

"Stephanie," Valerie said. "She's going to have a baby, and she's getting married."

My father was confused. He looked around the room. No Joe. No Ranger. His eyes locked on Diesel. "Not the psycho," he said.

Diesel blew out a sigh.

My father turned to my mother. "Get me the carving knife. Make sure it's sharp."

The doorbell rang again, and Lula and Connie rushed in with the cake. It was a huge wedding cake. Three tiers with a bride and groom on top.

"We got it," Lula said. "Mary Beth Krienski got cold feet and called off her wedding over the weekend, and we got this kick-ass bargain cake. Tasty Pastry was getting ready to heave it into the Dumpster. We got there just in time."

"It's yellow cake with lemon between the layers," Connie said.

"Put the cake on the dining room table," Grandma said. "Do I look okay for the pictures? Is my hair okay?"

Pictures! Val would want wedding pictures. "I didn't think to bring a camera," I said.

"That's okay," Valerie said. "I brought my camera."

"Yeah, and Connie and me stopped at the store and got one of them happy-snappy things," Lula said.

"You gotta have pictures of the bride," Grandma said.

All eyes turned to me. I'd gotten rushed out of the house this morning. I was still wearing the clothes I grabbed off the floor, and I had a ball cap on my head. And two big red hives on my face.

"That's okay, pumpkin," Diesel said to me. "I think you look . . . cute."

I introduced Annie and the justice of the peace, and Albert Kloughn broke out in a sweat.

"I thought I recognized you," he said to Annie. "We met just once, and it was a while ago."

Annie smiled at him. "It's so nice to see you again, Albert."

Albert was wearing a suit and tie, and he tugged at his shirt collar. "Can't breathe," he said.

"I'm in a hurry to get married," I yelled.

"We need to get some papers signed," Annie said. "Albert, you sign here as a witness. And Valerie. And here for Stephanie."

I watched Diesel sign. "Just Diesel?" I said to him. "No last name?"

"That's all I've got," Diesel said. "My name's Diesel."

"I need a bathroom," Albert said.

"No!" I told him. "You're gonna have to hold it. Everyone get in their places. Valerie, you stand next to me. And Albert, you stand next to Diesel."

The justice of the peace jumped into action and whipped out his little book with the ceremony in it.

Lula snapped a picture and my mother started crying.

Albert stood rooted to the spot, his face white but his cheeks stained red. Diesel grabbed Albert by the back of his suit jacket and dragged him to his side, so we were all four in a row.

"Are we ready to begin?" the justice asked.

"Yes," I said, "but we need to change places. This is actually going to be Valerie's and Albert's wedding."

Albert went down to his knees, and Diesel yanked him up to his feet, still holding tight to Albert's jacket.

The justice started reading from his script. "Dearly beloved—"

"Skip ahead to the *I do* part," I said to the justice.

The justice thumbed over a couple pages in his book.

"I'm going to be sick," Albert said.

"Dude," Diesel said. "Suck it up."

Albert went down to his knees again. "I got this thing about weddings."

"You were okay when you thought it was mine," Diesel said. "Just pretend it's mine."

"I can't pretend," Albert said. "I'm no good at pretending."

"We could have a double wedding," Valerie said. "Simultaneous. Then Albert could concentrate on being the best man."

I felt another hive break out on my chin. "I need my salve," I said. "Somebody get me some salve."

"It's not a bad idea," Annie said. "The universe would rest easier if Diesel was married."

"I'm *not* marrying Diesel!" I told Annie.

"Hey," Diesel said, "a lot of women would give anything to snag me."

"I'm not a lot of women."

"No shit," Diesel said. He shifted Albert from one hand to the other. "Can we get on with it? This guy's getting heavy."

"Would you really marry me?" I asked Diesel.

"Not forever, but a night might be fun."

Good grief.

"I'm confused," my father said. "Who's getting married?"

"Albert and Valerie are getting married," I said. I turned to Albert. "Here's the choice. You can go through this with your eyes open, or I can go get my stun gun, and you can get married with your eyes closed and your body twitching on the floor. My sister is pregnant again, and I'm going to make sure she's married."

Albert's mouth was open and his eyes were glazed.

"I'm going to take this as a choice to keep eyes open," I said to the justice of the peace. "Start reading. And hurry up."

"Do you—" the justice said to Albert.

"He does," we all said in unison.

"Me, too," Valerie said.

And Valerie and Albert were married.

"Let's cut the cake," Lula said.

My grandmother trotted in with a cake knife, and we clustered around the cake. It was a great cake, except Bob had eaten all the icing off one side.

"It's better this way," Grandma said. "You got a choice like white meat or dark meat, only this time it's icing or no icing."

I ran upstairs to the bathroom to look for more salve.

Diesel came up a minute later with a piece of cake for me. "That was a nice thing you did for your sister," Diesel said.

"How's Albert?"

"Deliriously happy."

"I think they've found true love."

Diesel nodded and fed me a piece of cake. "I have to go. I'm being reassigned."

"So soon?"

"Yeah, but I'll be back. You owe me a night."

"I do *not* owe you a night."

"I was willing to go the distance," Diesel said. "That has to be worth something."

"How about beer and pizza?"

"It's a start," Diesel said. "And don't worry about Delvina. I changed him into a toad."

The doorbell rang, and I heard Grandma hustle to get the door.

"Stephanie," she yelled up the stairs. "There's a flower delivery guy here, and he's got a bunch of flowers for you. The flower guy said two of these were supposed to go to your apartment, but I said you'd take them all here."

I went downstairs with Diesel following, and I took three boxes from Grandma.

The first box held a single perfect long-stemmed red rose. No card.

The second box held a dozen yellow roses. The message on the card was . . . LOVE, JOE.

The third box held a bouquet of daisies. The hand-scrawled note said . . . VALENTINE'S DAY SUCKS, USUALLY.

Valentine's Day didn't suck this year, I thought.

I felt someone brush a kiss across the nape of my neck, and I turned to Diesel, but the only thing behind me was the cake plate sitting on the bottom step.

JANET EVANOVICH

VISIONS OF SUGAR PLUMS

It's December in Jersey and Stephanie Plum has bigger problems
than the usual thugs, thieves and hoodlums. There's someone in her
apartment who just won't leave.

Sure, this sort of thing has happened to Stephanie before, but in the past
she's been able to talk her way out of trouble. This time, however, fast
talking, stun guns and pepper spray won't remove the intruder...

Visions of Sugar Plums takes Stephanie Plum on a Christmas holiday
adventure and introduces a new character that readers will adore. He's
as mysterious as Ranger, as sexy as Morelli, and ... well, we won't say
any more.

'Crime writing at its funniest' *Big Issue*

'All the easy class and wit that you expect to find in the best American
TV comedy, but too rarely find in modern fiction' *GQ*

He just wanted a decent book to read ...

Not too much to ask, is it? It was in 1935 when Allen Lane, Managing Director of Bodley Head Publishers, stood on a platform at Exeter railway station looking for something good to read on his journey back to London. His choice was limited to popular magazines and poor-quality paperbacks – the same choice faced every day by the vast majority of readers, few of whom could afford hardbacks. Lane's disappointment and subsequent anger at the range of books generally available led him to found a company – and change the world.

'We believed in the existence in this country of a vast reading public for intelligent books at a low price, and staked everything on it'
Sir Allen Lane, 1902–1970, founder of Penguin Books

The quality paperback had arrived – and not just in bookshops. Lane was adamant that his Penguins should appear in chain stores and tobacconists, and should cost no more than a packet of cigarettes.

Reading habits (and cigarette prices) have changed since 1935, but Penguin still believes in publishing the best books for everybody to enjoy. We still believe that good design costs no more than bad design, and we still believe that quality books published passionately and responsibly make the world a better place.

So wherever you see the little bird – whether it's on a piece of prize-winning literary fiction or a celebrity autobiography, political tour de force or historical masterpiece, a serial-killer thriller, reference book, world classic or a piece of pure escapism – you can bet that it represents the very best that the genre has to offer.

Whatever you like to read – trust Penguin.